PENGUIN BOOKS — GREAT IDEAS

Decline of the English Murder

George Orwell

1903–1950

George Orwell

Decline of the English Murder

PENGUIN BOOKS — GREAT IDEAS

PENGUIN BOOKS

Published by the Penguin Group
Penguin Books Ltd, 80 Strand, London WC2R ORL, England
Penguin Group (USA) Inc., 375 Hudson Street, New York, New York 10014, USA
Penguin Group (Canada), 90 Eglinton Avenue East, Suite 700, Toronto, Ontario, Canada M4P 2Y3
(a division of Pearson Penguin Canada Inc.)
Penguin Ireland, 25 St Stephen's Green, Dublin 2, Ireland
(a division of Penguin Books Ltd)
Penguin Group (Australia), 250 Camberwell Road, Camberwell, Victoria 3124, Australia
(a division of Pearson Australia Group Pty Ltd)
Penguin Books India Pvt Ltd, 11 Community Centre, Panchsheel Park, New Delhi – 110 017, India
Penguin Group (NZ), 67 Apollo Drive, Rosedale, North Shore 0632, New Zealand
(a division of Pearson New Zealand Ltd)
Penguin Books (South Africa) (Pty) Ltd, 24 Sturdee Avenue,
Rosebank, Johannesburg 2196, South Africa

Penguin Books Ltd, Registered Offices: 80 Strand, London WC2R ORL, England

www.penguin.com

'Clink' written August 1932
'Decline of the English Murder' first published in *Tribune*, 15 February 1946
'Just Junk – But Who Could Resist It?' first published as the Saturday Essay, *Evening Standard*,
5 January 1946
'Good Bad Books' first published in *Tribune*, 2 November 1945
'Boys' Weeklies' first published in *Horizon*, March 1940
'Women's Twopenny Papers' extract from 'As I Please' first published in *Tribune*, 28 July 1944
'The Art of Donald McGill' first published in *Horizon*, September 1941
'Hop-Picking Diary', written 25 August to 8 October 1931
This selection first published in Penguin Books 2009

009

Copyright © the Estate of Sonia Brownell Orwell, 1984
All rights reserved

Set by Rowland Phototypesetting Ltd, Bury St Edmunds, Suffolk
Printed in England by Clays Ltd, Elcograf S.p.A.

978-0-141-19126-3

www.greenpenguin.co.uk

MIX
Paper from
responsible sources
FSC® C018179

Penguin Books is committed to a sustainable
future for our business, our readers and our planet.
This book is made from Forest Stewardship
Council™ certified paper.

Contents

Clink

This trip was a failure, as the object of it was to get into prison, and I did not, in fact, get more than forty-eight hours in custody; however, I am recording it, as the procedure in the police court etc. was fairly interesting. I am writing this eight months after it happened, so am not certain of any dates, but it all happened a week or ten days before Xmas 1931.

I started out on Saturday afternoon with four or five shillings, and went out to the Mile End Road, because my plan was to get drunk and incapable, and I thought they would be less lenient towards drunkards in the East End. I bought some tobacco and a 'Yank Mag' against my forthcoming imprisonment, and then, as soon as the pubs opened, went and had four or five pints, topping up with a quarter bottle of whisky, which left me with twopence in hand. By the time the whisky was low in the bottle I was tolerably drunk – more drunk than I had intended, for it happened that I had eaten nothing all day, and the alcohol acted quickly on my empty stomach. It was all I could do to stand upright, though my brain was quite clear – with me, when I am drunk, my brain remains clear long after my legs and speech have gone. I began staggering along the pavement in a westward direction, and for a long time did not meet any policemen, though the streets were crowded and all the people pointed and laughed at me. Finally I saw two policemen coming. I pulled the whisky bottle out of my pocket and, in their sight, drank what was left, which nearly knocked me out, so that I clutched a lamp-post and fell down. The two policemen ran towards me, turned me over and took the bottle out of my hand.

THEY: 'Ere, what you bin drinking? (*For a moment they may have thought it was a case of suicide.*)

I: Thass my boll whisky. You lea' me alone.

THEY: Coo, 'e's fair bin bathing in it! – What you bin doing of, eh?

I: Bin in boozer 'avin' bit o' fun. Christmas, ain't it?

THEY: No, not by a week it ain't. You got mixed up in the dates, you 'ave. You better come along with us. We'll look after yer.

I: Why sh'd I come along you?

THEY: Jest so's we'll look after you and make you comfortable. You'll get run over, rolling about like that.

I: Look. Boozer over there. Less go in 'ave drink.

THEY: You've 'ad enough for one night, ole chap. You best come with us.

I: Where you takin' me?

THEY: Jest somewhere as you'll get a nice quiet kip with a clean sheet and two blankets and all.

I: Shall I get drink there?

THEY: Course you will. Got a boozer on the premises, we 'ave.

All this while they were leading me gently along the pavement. They had my arms in the grip (I forget what it is called) by which you can break a man's arm with one twist, but they were as gentle with me as though I had been a child. I was internally quite sober, and it amused me very much to see the cunning way in which they persuaded me along, never once disclosing the fact that we were making for the police station. This is, I suppose, the usual procedure with drunks.

When we got to the station (it was Bethnal Green, but I did not learn this till Monday) they dumped me in a chair & began emptying my pockets while the sergeant questioned me. I pretended, however, to be too drunk to give sensible answers, & he told them in disgust to take me off to the cells, which they did. The cell was about the same size as a Casual Ward cell (about 10 ft. by 5 ft. by 10 ft. high), but much cleaner & better appointed. It was made of white porcelain bricks, and was furnished with a W. C., a hot water pipe, a plank bed, a horsehair pillow and two blankets. There was a tiny barred window high up near the roof, and an electric bulb behind a guard of thick glass was kept burning all night. The door was steel, with the usual spy-hole and aperture for serving food through. The constables in searching me had taken away my money, matches, razor, and also my scarf – this, I learned afterwards, because prisoners have been known to hang themselves on their scarves.

There is very little to say about the next day and night, which were unutterably boring. I was horribly sick, sicker than I have ever been from a bout of drunkenness, no doubt from having an empty stomach. During Sunday I was given two meals of bread and marg. and tea (spike quality), and one of meat and potatoes – this, I believe, owing to the kindness of the sergeant's wife, for I think only bread and marg, is provided for prisoners in the lock-up. I was not allowed to shave, and there was only a little cold water to wash in. When the charge sheet was filled up I told the story I always tell, viz. that my name was Edward Burton, and my parents kept a cake-shop in Blythburgh, where I had been employed as a clerk in a draper's shop; that I had had the sack for drunkenness, and my parents, finally getting sick of my drunken habits, had turned me adrift. I added that I had been working as an outside porter at Billingsgate, and having unexpectedly 'knocked up' six shillings on Saturday, had gone on the razzle. The police were quite kind, and read me lectures on drunkenness, with the usual stuff about seeing that I still had some good in me etc. etc. They offered to let me out on bail on my own recognizance, but I had no money and nowhere to go, so I elected to stay in custody. It was very dull, but I had my 'Yank Mag', and could get a smoke if I asked the constable on duty in the passage for a light – prisoners are not allowed matches, of course.

The next morning very early they turned me out of my cell to wash, gave me back my scarf, and took me out into the yard and put me in the Black Maria. Inside, the Black Maria was just like a French public lavatory, with a row of tiny locked compartments on either side, each just large enough to sit down in. People had scrawled their names, offences and the lengths of their sentences all over the walls of my compartment; also, several times, variants on this couplet –

> Detective Smith knows how to gee;
> Tell him he's a cunt from me.

('Gee' in this context means to act as an agent provocateur.) We drove round to various stations picking up about ten prisoners in all, until the Black Maria was quite full. They were quite a jolly crowd inside. The compartment doors were open at the top, for ventilation, so that you could reach across, and somebody had managed to smuggle matches in, and we all had a smoke. Presently we began singing, and, as it was near Christmas sang several carols. We drove up to Old Street Police Court singing –

> Adeste, fideles, laeti triumphantes,
> Adeste, adeste ad Bethlehem, etc.

which seemed to me rather inappropriate.

At the police court they took me off and put me in a cell identical with the one at Bethnal Green, even to having the same number of bricks in it – I counted in each case. There were three men in the cell beside myself. One was a smartly dressed, florid, well-set-up man of about thirty five, whom I would have taken for a commercial traveller or perhaps a bookie, and another a middle-aged Jew, also quite decently dressed. The other man was evidently a habitual burglar. He was a short rough-looking man with grey hair and a worn face, and at this moment in such a state of agitation over his approaching trial that he could not keep still an instant. He kept pacing up and down the cell like a wild beast, brushing against our knees as we sat on the plank bed, and exclaiming that he was innocent – he was charged, apparently, with loitering with intent to commit burglary. He said that he had nine previous convictions against him, and that in these cases, which are mainly of suspicion, old offenders are nearly always convicted. From time to time he would shake his fist towards the door and exclaim 'Fucking toe-rag! Fucking toe-rag!', meaning the 'split' who had arrested him.

Presently two more prisoners were put into the cell, an ugly Belgian youth charged with obstructing traffic with a barrow, and an extraordinary hairy creature who was either deaf and dumb or spoke no English. Except this last all the prisoners talked about their cases with the utmost freedom. The florid, smart man, it appeared, was a public house 'guv'nor' (it is a sign of how utterly the London publicans are in the claw of the brewers that they are always referred to as 'governors', not 'landlords'; being, in fact, no better than employees), & had embezzled the Christmas Club money. As usual, he was head over ears in debt to the brewers, and no doubt had taken some of the money in hopes of backing a winner. Two of the subscribers had discovered this a few days before the money was due to be paid out, and laid an information. The 'guv'nor' immediately paid back all save £12, which was also refunded before his case came up for trial. Nevertheless, he was certain to be sentenced, as the magistrates are hard on these cases – he did, in fact, get four months later in the day. He was ruined for life, of course. The brewers would file bankruptcy proceedings and sell up all his stock and furniture, and he would never be given a pub licence again. He was trying to brazen it out in front of the rest of us, and smoking cigarettes incessantly from a stock of Gold Flake packets he had laid in – the last time in his life, I dare say, that he would have quite enough cigarettes. There was a staring, abstracted look in his eyes all the time while he talked. I think the fact that his life was at an end, as far as any decent position in society went, was gradually sinking into him. HOW DID GEORGE KNOW?

The Jew had been a buyer at Smithfields for a kosher butcher. After working seven years for the same employer he suddenly misappropriated £28, went up to Edinburgh – I don't know why Edinburgh – and had a 'good time' with tarts, and came back and surrendered himself when the money was gone. £16 of the money had been repaid, and the rest was to be repaid by monthly instalments. He had a wife and a number of children. He told us, what interested me, that his employer would probably get into trouble at the synagogue for prosecuting him. It appears that the Jews have arbitration courts of their own, & a Jew is not supposed to prosecute another Jew, at least in a breach of trust case like this, without first submitting it to the arbitration court.

One remark made by these men struck me – I heard it from almost every prisoner who was up for a serious offence. It was, 'It's not the prison I mind, it's losing my job.' This is, I believe, symptomatic of the dwindling power of the law compared with that of the capitalist.

They kept us waiting several hours. It was very uncomfortable in the cell, for there was not room for all of us to sit down on the plank bed, and it was beastly cold in spite of the number of us. Several of the men used the W.C., which was disgusting in so small a cell, especially as the plug did not work. The publican distributed his cigarettes generously, the constable in the passage supplying lights. From time to time an extraordinary clanking noise came from the cell next door, where a youth who had stabbed his 'tart' in the stomach – she was likely to recover, we heard – was locked up alone. Goodness knows what was happening, but it sounded as though he were chained to the wall. At about ten they gave us each a mug of tea – this, it appeared, not provided by the authorities but by the police court missionaries – and shortly afterwards shepherded us along to a sort of large waiting room where the prisoners awaited trial.

There were perhaps fifty prisoners here, men of every type, but on the whole much more smartly dressed than one would expect. They were strolling up and down with their hats on, shivering with the cold. I saw here a thing which interested me greatly. When I was being taken to my cell I had seen two dirty-looking ruffians, much dirtier than myself and presumably drunks or obstruction cases, being put into another cell in the row. Here, in the waiting room, these two were at work with note-books in their hands, interrogating prisoners. It appeared that they were 'splits', and were put into the cells disguised as prisoners, to pick up any information that was going – for there is complete freemasonry between prisoners, and they talk without reserve in front of one another. It was a dingy trick, I thought.

All the while the prisoners were being taken by ones & twos along a corridor to the court. Presently a sergeant shouted 'Come on the drunks!' and four or five of us filed along the corridor and stood waiting at the entrance of the court. A young constable on duty there advised me –

'Take your cap off when you go in, plead guilty and don't give back answers. Got any previous convictions?'

'No.'

'Six bob you'll get. Going to pay it?'

'I can't, I've only twopence.'

'Ah well, it don't matter. Lucky for you Mr Brown isn't on the bench this morning. Teetotaller he is. He don't half give it to the drunks. Cool!'

The drunk cases were dealt with so rapidly that I had not even time to notice what the court was like. I only had a vague impression of a raised platform with a coat of arms over it, clerks sitting at tables below, and a railing. We filed past the railing like people passing through a turnstile, & the proceedings in each case sounded like this –

'Edward-Burton-drunk-and-incapable-Drunk?-Yes-Six-shillings-move-on-NEXT!'

All this in the space of about five seconds. At the other side of the court we reached a room where a sergeant was sitting at a desk with a ledger.

'Six shillings?' he said.

'Yes.'

'Going to pay it?'

'I can't.'

'All right, back you go to your cell.'

And they took me back and locked me in the cell from which I had come, about ten minutes after I had left it.

The publican had also been brought back, his case having been postponed, and the Belgian youth, who, like me, could not pay his fine. The Jew was gone, whether released or sentenced we did not know. Throughout the day prisoners were coming and going, some waiting trial, some until the Black Maria was available to take them off to prison. It was cold, and the nasty faecal stench in the cell became unbearable. They gave us our dinner at about two o'clock – it consisted of a mug of tea and two slices of bread and marg. for each man. Apparently this was the regulation meal. One could, if one had friends outside get food sent in, but it struck me as damnably unfair that a penniless man must face his trial with only bread and marg. in his belly; also unshaven – I, at this time, had had no chance of shaving for over forty-eight hours – which is likely to prejudice the magistrates against him. 1932

Among the prisoners who were put temporarily in the cell were two friends or partners named apparently Snouter and Charlie, who had been arrested for some street offence – obstruction with a barrow, I dare say. Snouter was a thin, red-faced, malignant-looking man, and Charlie a short, powerful, jolly man. Their conversation was rather interesting.

CHARLIE: Cripes, it ain't 'alf fucking cold in 'ere. Lucky for us ole Brown ain't on to-day. Give you a month as soon as look at yer.

SNOUTER (bored, and singing):

> Tap, tap, tapetty-tap,
> I'm a perfect devil at that;
> Tapping 'em 'ere, tapping 'em there,
> *I* bin tapping 'em everywhere

CHARLIE: Oh, fuck off with yer tapping! Scrumping's what yer want this time of year. All them rows of turkeys in the winders, like rows of fucking soldiers with no clo'es on – don't it make yer fucking mouth water to look at 'em. Bet yer a tanner I 'ave one of 'em afore tonight.

SNOUTER: What's 'a good? Can't cook the bugger over the kip-'ouse fire, can you?

CHARLIE: Oo wants to cook it? I know where I can flog (sell) it for a bob or two, though.

SNOUTER: 'Sno good. Chantin's the game this time of year. Carols. Fair twist their 'earts round, I can, when I get on the mournful. Old tarts weep their fucking eyes out when they 'ear me. I won't 'alf give them a doing this Christmas. I'll kip indoors if I 'ave to cut it out of their bowels.

CHARLIE: Ah, *I* can sling you a bit of a carol. 'Ymns, too. (*He begins singing in a good bass voice*) –

> Jesu, lover of my soul,
> Let me to thy bosom fly –

THE CONSTABLE ON DUTY (*looking through the grille*): Nah then, in 'ere, nah then! What yer think this is? Baptist prayer meeting?

CHARLIE (*in a low voice as the constable disappears*): Fuck off, pisspot. (*He hums*) –

> While the gathering waters roll,
> While the tempest still is 'igh!

You won't find many in the 'ymnal as I can't sling you. Sung bass in the choir my last two years in Dartmoor, I did.

SNOUTER: Ah? Wassit like in Dartmoor now? D'you get jam now?

CHARLIE: Not jam. Gets cheese, though, twice a week.

SNOUTER: Ah? 'Ow long was you doing?

CHARLIE: Four year.

SNOUTER: Four years without cunt – Cripes! Fellers inside'd go 'alf mad if they saw a pair of legs [a woman], eh?

CHARLIE: Ah well, in Dartmoor we used to fuck old women down on the allotments. Take 'em under the 'edge in the mist. Spud-grabbers they was – ole trots seventy year old. Forty of us was caught and went through 'ell for it. Bread and water, chains – everythink. I took my Bible oath as I wouldn't get no more stretches after that.

SNOUTER: Yes, you! 'Ow come you got in the stir lars' time then?

CHARLIE: You wouldn't 'ardly believe it, boy. I was narked – narked by my own sister! Yes, my own fucking sister. My sister's a cow if ever there was one. She got married to a religious maniac, and 'e's so fucking religious that she's got fifteen kids now. Well, it was 'im put 'er up to narking me. But I got it back on 'em *I* can tell you. What do you think I done first thing, when I come out of the stir? I bought a 'ammer, and I went round to my sister's 'ouse and smashed 'er piano to fucking matchwood. I did. 'There,' I says, 'that's what you get for narking me! You mare,' I says etc. etc. etc.

This kind of conversation went on more or less all day between these two, who were only in for some petty offence & quite pleased with themselves. Those who were going to prison were silent and restless, and the look on some of the men's faces – respectable men under arrest for the first time – was dreadful. They took the publican out at about three in the afternoon, to be sent off to prison. He had cheered up a little on learning from the constable on duty that he was going to the same prison as Lord Kylsant. He thought that by sucking up to Lord K. in jail he might get a job from him when he came out.

I had no idea how long I was going to be incarcerated, & supposed that it would be several days at least. However, between four and five o'clock they took me out of the cell, gave back the things which had been confiscated, and shot me into the street forthwith. Evidently the day in custody served instead of the fine. I had only twopence and had had nothing to eat all day except bread and marg., and was damnably hungry; however, as always happens when it is a choice between tobacco and food, I bought tobacco with my twopence. Then I went down to the Church Army shelter in the Waterloo Road, where you get a kip, two meals of bread and corned beef and tea and a prayer meeting, for four hours work at sawing wood.

The next morning I went home, got some money, and went out to Edmonton. I turned up at the Casual Ward about nine at night, not downright drunk but more or less under the influence, thinking this would lead to prison – for it is an offence under the Vagrancy Act for a tramp to come drunk to the Casual Ward. The porter, however, treated me with great consideration, evidently feeling that a tramp with money enough to buy drink ought to be respected. During the next few days I made several more attempts to get into trouble by begging under the noses of the police, but I seemed to bear a charmed life – no one took any notice of me. So, as I did not want to do anything serious which might lead to investigations about my identity etc., I gave it up. The trip, therefore, was more or less of a failure, but I have recorded it as a fairly interesting experience.

Decline of the English Murder

It is Sunday afternoon, preferably before the war. The wife is already asleep in the armchair, and the children have been sent out for a nice long walk. You put your feet up on the sofa, settle your spectacles on your nose, and open the *News of the World*. Roast beef and Yorkshire, or roast pork and apple sauce, followed up by suet pudding and driven home, as it were, by a cup of mahogany-brown tea, have put you in just the right mood. Your pipe is drawing sweetly, the sofa cushions are soft underneath you, the fire is well alight, the air is warm and stagnant. In these blissful circumstances, what is it that you want to read about?

Naturally, about a murder. But what kind of murder? If one examines the murders which have given the greatest amount of pleasure to the British public, the murders whose story is known in its general outline to almost everyone and which have been made into novels and rehashed over and over again by the Sunday papers, one finds a fairly strong family resemblance running through the greater number of them. Our great period in murder, our Elizabethan period, so to speak, seems to have been between roughly 1850 and 1925; and the murderers whose reputation has stood the test of time are the following: Dr Palmer of Rugeley, Jack the Ripper, Neill Cream, Mrs Maybrick, Dr Crippen, Seddon, Joseph

Smith, Armstrong, and Bywaters and Thompson. In addition, in 1919 or thereabouts, there was another very celebrated case which fits into the general pattern but which I had better not mention by name, because the accused man was acquitted.

Of the above-mentioned nine cases, at least four have had successful novels based on them, one has been made into a popular melodrama, and the amount of literature surrounding them, in the form of newspaper write-ups, criminological treatises and reminiscences by lawyers and police officers, would make a considerable library. It is difficult to believe that any recent English crime will be remembered so long and so intimately, and not only because the violence of external events has made murder seem unimportant, but because the prevalent type of crime seems to be changing. The principal *cause célèbre* of the war years was the so-called Cleft Chin Murder, which has now been written up in a popular booklet; the verbatim account of the trial was published some time last year by Messrs Jarrolds with an introduction by Mr Bechhofer-Roberts. Before returning to this pitiful and sordid case, which is only interesting from a socio-logical and perhaps a legal point of view, let me try to define what it is that the readers of Sunday papers mean when they say fretfully that 'you never seem to get a good murder nowadays'.

In considering the nine murders I named above, one can start by excluding the Jack the Ripper case, which is in a class by itself. Of the other eight, six were poisoning cases, and eight of the ten criminals belonged to the middle class. In one way or another, sex was a powerful motive in all but two cases, and in at least four cases respectability – the desire to gain a secure position in life, or not to forfeit one's social position by some scandal such as a divorce – was one of the main reasons for committing murder. In more than half the cases, the object was to get hold of a certain known sum of money such as a legacy or an insurance policy, but the amount involved was nearly always small. In most of the cases the crime only came to light slowly, as the result of careful investigation which started off with the suspicions of neighbours or relatives; and in nearly every case there was some dramatic coincidence, in which the finger of Providence could be clearly seen, or one of those episodes that no novelist would dare to make up, such as Crippen's flight across the Atlantic with his mistress dressed as a boy, or Joseph Smith playing 'Nearer, my God, to Thee' on the harmonium while one of his wives was drowning in the next room. The background of all these crimes, except Neill Cream's, was essentially domestic; of twelve victims, seven were either wife or husband of the murderer.

With all this in mind one can construct what would be, from a *News of the World* reader's point of view, the 'perfect' murder. The murderer should be a little man of the professional class – a dentist or a solicitor, say – living an intensely respectable life somewhere in the suburbs, and preferably in a semi-detached house, which will allow the neighbours to hear suspicious sounds through the wall. He should be either chairman of the local Conservative Party branch, or a leading Nonconformist and strong Temperance advocate. He should go astray through cherishing a guilty passion for his secretary or the wife of a rival professional man, and should only bring himself to the point of murder after long and terrible wrestles with his conscience. Having decided on murder, he should plan it all with the utmost cunning, and only slip up over some tiny, unforeseeable detail. The means chosen should, of course, be poison. In the last analysis he should commit murder because this seems to him less disgraceful, and less damaging to his career, than being detected in adultery. With this kind of background, a crime can have dramatic and even tragic qualities which make it memorable and excite pity for both victim and murderer. Most of the crimes mentioned above have a touch of this atmosphere, and in three cases, including the one I referred to but did not name, the story approximates to the one I have outlined.

Now compare the Cleft Chin Murder. There is no depth of feeling in it. It was almost chance that the two people concerned committed that particular murder, and it was only by good luck that they did not commit several others. The background was not domesticity, but the anonymous life of the dance halls and the false values of the American film. The two culprits were an eighteen-year-old ex-waitress named Elizabeth Jones, and an American army deserter, posing as an officer, named Karl Hulten. They were only together for six days, and it seems doubtful whether, until they were arrested, they even learned one another's true names. They met casually in a teashop, and that night went out for a ride in a stolen army truck. Jones described herself as a strip-tease artist, which was not strictly true (she had given one unsuccessful performance in this line), and declared that she wanted to do something dangerous, 'like being a gun-moll'. Hulten described himself as a big-time Chicago gangster, which was also untrue. They met a girl bicycling along the road, and to show how tough he was Hulten ran over her with his truck, after which the pair robbed her of the few shillings that were on her. On another occasion they knocked out a girl to whom they had offered a lift, took her coat and handbag and threw her into a river. Finally, in the most wanton way, they murdered a taxi-driver who happened to have £8 in his pocket. Soon afterwards they parted. Hulten was caught because he had foolishly kept the dead man's car, and Jones made spontaneous confessions to the police. In court each prisoner incriminated the other. In between crimes, both of them seem to have behaved with the utmost callousness: they spent the dead taxi-driver's £8 at the dog races.

Judging from her letters, the girl's case has a certain amount of psychological interest, but this murder probably captured the headlines because it provided distraction amid the doodle-bugs and the anxieties of the Battle of France. Jones and Hulten committed their murder to the tune of V1, and were convicted to the tune of V2. There was also considerable excitement because – as has become usual in England – the man was sentenced to death and the girl to imprisonment.

According to Mr Raymond, the reprieving of Jones caused widespread indignation and streams of telegrams to the Home Secretary: in her native town, 'She should hang' was chalked on the walls beside pictures of a

· figure dangling from a gallows. Considering that only ten women have been hanged in Britain in this century, and that the practice has gone out largely because of popular feeling against it, it is difficult not to feel that this clamour to hang an eighteen-year-old girl was due partly to the brutalizing effects of war. Indeed, the whole meaningless story, with its atmosphere of dance-halls, movie palaces, cheap perfume, false names and stolen cars, belongs essentially to a war period.

Perhaps it is significant that the most talked-of English murder of recent years should have been committed by an American and an English girl who had become partly americanized. But it is difficult to believe that this case will be so long remembered as the old domestic poisoning dramas, product of a stable society where the all-prevailing hypocrisy did at least ensure that crimes as serious as murder should have strong emotions behind them

Just Junk – But Who Could Resist It?

Which is the most attractive junk shop in London is a matter of taste, or for debate: but I could lead you to some first-rate ones in the dingier areas of Greenwich, in Islington near the Angel, in Holloway, in Paddington, and in the hinterland of the Edgware Road. Except for a couple near Lord's – and even those are in a section of street that happens to have fallen into decay – I have never seen a junk shop worth a second glance in what is called a 'good' neighbourhood.

A junk shop is not to be confused with an antique shop. An antique shop is clean, its goods are attractively set out and priced at about double their value and once inside the shop you are usually bullied into buying something.

A junk shop has a fine film of dust over the window, its stock may include literally anything that is not perishable, and its proprietor, who is usually asleep in a small room at the back, displays no eagerness to make a sale.

Also, its finest treasures are never discoverable at first glimpse; they have to be sorted out from among a medley of bamboo cake-stands, Britannia-ware dish-covers, turnip watches, dog-eared books, ostrich eggs, typewriters of extinct makes, spectacles without lenses, decanters without stoppers, stuffed birds, wire fire guards, bunches of keys, boxes of nuts and bolts, conch shells from the Indian Ocean, boot trees, Chinese ginger jars and pictures of Highland cattle.

Some of the things to look out for in the junk shop are Victorian brooches and lockets of agate or other semi-precious stones.

Perhaps five out of six of these things are hideously ugly, but there are also very beautiful objects among them. They are set in silver, or more often in pinchbeck, a charming alloy which for some reason is no longer made.

Other things worth looking for are papier-mâché snuffboxes with pictures painted on the lid, lustre-ware jugs, muzzle-loading pistols made round about 1830 and ships in bottles. These are still made, but the old ones are always the best, because of the elegant shape of the Victorian bottles and the delicate green of the glass.

Or, again, musical boxes, horse brasses, copper powder-horns, Jubilee mugs (for some reason the 1887 Jubilee produced much pleasanter keep-sakes than the Diamond Jubilee ten years later) and glass paper-weights with pictures at the bottom.

There are others that have a piece of coral enclosed in the glass, but these are always fantastically expensive. Or you may come across a scrap book full of Victorian fashion-plates and pressed flowers or even, if you are exceptionally lucky, the scrap book's big brother, a scrap screen.

Scrap screens – all too rare nowadays – are simply ordinary wooden or canvas screens with coloured scraps cut out and pasted all over them in such a way as to make more or less coherent pictures. The best were made round about 1880, but if you buy one at a junk shop it is sure to be defective, and the great charm of owning such a screen lies in patching it up yourself.

You can use coloured reproductions from art magazines, Christmas cards, postcards, advertisements, book jackets, even cigarette cards. There is always room for one more scrap, and with careful placing anything can be made to look congruous.

Thus, merely in one corner of my own scrap screen, Cézanne's card-players with a black bottle between them are impinging on a street scene in medieval Florence, while on the other side of the street one of Gauguin's South Sea islanders is sitting beside an English lake where a lady in leg-of-mutton sleeves is paddling a canoe. They all look perfectly at home together.

All these things are curiosities, but one does find useful things in the junk shop as well.

In a shop in Kentish Town, since blitzed, I once bought an old French sword-bayonet, price sixpence, which did four years' service as a fire-poker. And during the last few years the junk shop has been the only place where you could buy certain carpentering tools – a jack plane for instance – or such useful objects as corkscrews, clock keys, skates, wine glasses, copper saucepans and spare pram wheels.

In some shops you can find keys to fit almost any lock, others specialize in pictures and are therefore useful when you need a frame. Indeed, I have often found that the cheapest way of buying a frame is to buy a picture and then throw away the picture.

But the attraction of the junk shop does not lie solely

in the bargains you pick up, nor even in the aesthetic value which – at a generous estimate – 5 per cent of its contents may possess. Its appeal is to the jackdaw inside all of us, the instinct that makes a child hoard copper nails, clock springs and the glass marbles out of lemonade bottles. To get pleasure out of a junk shop you are not obliged to buy anything, nor even to want to buy anything.

I know a shop in Tottenham Court road where I have never, over a period of many years, seen anything that was not offensively ugly and another, not far from Baker-street, where there is nearly always something tempting. The first appeals to me almost as strongly as the second.

Another shop, in the Chalk Farm area, sells nothing but rubbishy fragments of old metal. For as long as I can remember the same worn-out tools and lengths of lead piping have been lying in the trays, the same gas stoves have been mouldering in the doorway. I have never bought anything there, never even seen anything that I contemplated buying. Yet it would be all but impossible for me to pass that way without crossing the street to have a good look.

Good Bad Books

1945

Not long ago a publisher commissioned me to write an introduction for a reprint of a novel by Leonard Merrick. This publishing house, it appears, is going to reissue a long series of minor and partly forgotten novels of the twentieth century. It is a valuable service in these book-less days, and I rather envy the person whose job it will be to scout round the threepenny boxes, hunting down copies of his boyhood favourites.

A type of book which we hardly seem to produce in these days, but which flowered with great richness in the late nineteenth and early twentieth centuries, is what Chesterton called the 'good bad book': that is, the kind of book that has no literary pretensions but which remains readable when more serious productions have perished. Obviously outstanding books in this line are *Raffles* and the Sherlock Holmes stories, which have kept their place when innumerable 'problem novels', 'human documents' and 'terrible indictments' of this or that have fallen into deserved oblivion. (Who has worn better, Conan Doyle or Meredith?) Almost in the same class as these I put R. Austin Freeman's earlier stories – 'The Singing Bone', 'The Eye of Osiris' and others – Ernest Bramah's *Max Carrados*, and, dropping the standard a bit, Guy Boothby's Tibetan thriller, *Dr Nikola*, a sort of schoolboy version of Huc's *Travels in Tartary* which would probably make a real visit to Central Asia seem a dismal anticlimax.

But apart from thrillers, there were the minor humorous writers of the period. For example, Pett Ridge – but I admit his full-length books no longer seem readable – E. Nesbit (*The Treasure Seekers*), George Birmingham, who was good so long as he kept off politics, the pornographic Binstead ('Pitcher' of the *Pink 'Un*), and, if American books can be included, Booth Tarkington's Penrod stories. A cut above most of these was Barry Pain. Some of Pain's humorous writings are, I suppose, still in print, but to anyone who comes across it I recommend what must now be a very rare book – *The Octave of Claudius*, a brilliant exercise in the macabre. Somewhat later in time there was Peter Blundell, who wrote in the W. W. Jacobs vein about Far Eastern seaport towns, and who seems to be rather unaccountably forgotten, in spite of having been praised in print by H. G. Wells.

However, all the books I have been speaking of are frankly 'escape' literature. They form pleasant patches in one's memory, quiet corners where the mind can browse at odd moments, but they hardly pretend to have anything to do with real life. There is another kind of good bad book which is more seriously intended, and which tells us, I think, something about the nature of the novel and the reasons for its present decadence. During the last fifty years there has been a whole series of writers – some of them are still writing – whom it is quite impossible to call 'good' by any strictly literary standard, but who are natural novelists and who seem to attain sincerity partly because they are not inhibited

by good taste. In this class I put Leonard Merrick himself,
W. L. George, J. D. Beresford, Ernest Raymond, May
Sinclair, and – at a lower level than the others but still
essentially similar – A. S. M. Hutchinson.

Most of these have been prolific writers, and their
output has naturally varied in quality. I am thinking in
each case of one or two outstanding books: for example,
Merrick's *Cynthia*, J. D. Beresford's *A Candidate for Truth*,
W. L. George's *Caliban*, May Sinclair's *The Combined
Maze* and Ernest Raymond's *We, the Accused*. In each of
these books the author has been able to identify himself
with his imagined characters, to feel with them and
invite sympathy on their behalf, with a kind of abandon-
ment that cleverer people would find it difficult to
achieve. They bring out the fact that intellectual refinement can be a disadvantage to a story-teller, as it would
be to a music-hall comedian.

Take, for example, Ernest Raymond's *We, the Accused*
– a peculiarly sordid and convincing murder story, probably based on the Crippen case. I think it gains a great
deal from the fact that the author only partly grasps the
pathetic vulgarity of the people he is writing about, and
therefore does not despise them. Perhaps it even – like
Theodore Dreiser's *An American Tragedy* – gains something from the clumsy long-winded manner in which it
is written; detail is piled on detail, with almost no attempt
at selection, and in the process an effect of terrible,
grinding cruelty is slowly built up. So also with *A Candidate for Truth*. Here there is not the same clumsiness, but
there is the same ability to take seriously the problems
of commonplace people. So also with *Cynthia* and at any

rate the earlier part of *Caliban*. The greater part of what
W. L. George wrote was shoddy rubbish, but in this
particular book, based on the career of Northcliffe, he
achieved some memorable and truthful pictures of
lower-middle-class London life. Parts of this book are
probably autobiographical, and one of the advantages
of good bad writers is their lack of shame in writing
autobiography. Exhibitionism and self-pity are the bane
of the novelist, and yet if he is too frightened of them
his creative gift may suffer.

The existence of good bad literature – the fact that
one can be amused or excited or even moved by a book
that one's intellect simply refuses to take seriously – is a
reminder that art is not the same thing as cerebration. I
imagine that by any test that could be devised, Carlyle
would be found to be a more intelligent man than Trollope. Yet Trollope has remained readable and Carlyle has
not: with all his cleverness he had not even the wit to write
in plain straightforward English. In novelists, almost as
much as in poets, the connexion between intelligence and
creative power is hard to establish. A good novelist may
be a prodigy of self-discipline like Flaubert, or he may be
an intellectual sprawl like Dickens. Enough talent to set
up dozens of ordinary writers has been poured into
Wyndham Lewis's so-called novels, such as *Tarr* or
Snooty Baronet. Yet it would be a very heavy labour to
read one of these books right through. Some indefinable
quality, a sort of literary vitamin, which exists even in a
book like *If Winter Comes*, is absent from them.

Perhaps the supreme example of the 'good bad' book
is *Uncle Tom's Cabin*. It is an unintentionally ludicrous

book, full of preposterous melodramatic incidents; it is also deeply moving and essentially true; it is hard to say which quality outweighs the other. But *Uncle Tom's Cabin*, after all, is trying to be serious and to deal with the real world. How about the frankly escapist writers, the purveyors of thrills and 'light' humour? How about *Sherlock Holmes*, *Vice Versa*, *Dracula*, *Helen's Babies* or *King Solomon's Mines*? All of these are definitely absurd books, books which one is more inclined to laugh *at* than *with*, and which were hardly taken seriously even by their authors; yet they have survived, and will probably continue to do so. All one can say is that, while civilization remains such that one needs distraction from time to time, 'light' literature has its appointed place; also that there is such a thing as sheer skill, or native grace, which may have more survival value than erudition or intellectual power. There are music-hall songs which are better poems than three quarters of the stuff that gets into the anthologies:

> Come where the booze is cheaper,
> Come where the pots hold more,
> Come where the boss is a bit of a sport,
> Come to the pub next door!

Or again:

> Two lovely black eyes –
> Oh, what a surprise!
> Only for calling another man wrong,
> Two lovely black eyes!

I would far rather have written either of these than, say, 'The Blessed Damozel' or 'Love in the Valley'. And by the same token I would back *Uncle Tom's Cabin* to outlive the complete works of Virginia Woolf or George Moore, though I know of no strictly literary test which would show where the superiority lies.

Boys' Weeklies

You never walk through any poor quarter in any big town without coming upon a small newsagent's shop. The general appearance of these shops is always very much the same: a few posters for the *Daily Mail* and the *News of the World* outside, a poky little window with sweet-bottles and packets of Players, and a dark interior smelling of liquorice allsorts and festooned from floor to ceiling with vilely printed twopenny papers, most of them with lurid cover illustrations in three colours.

Except for the daily and evening papers, the stock of these shops hardly overlaps at all with that of the big newsagents. Their main selling line is the twopenny weekly, and the number and variety of these are almost unbelievable. Every hobby and pastime – cage-birds, fretwork, carpentering, bees, carrier-pigeons, home conjuring, philately, chess – has at least one paper devoted to it, and generally several. Gardening and livestock-keeping must have at least a score between them. Then there are the sporting papers, the radio papers, the children's comics, the various snippet papers such as *Tit-Bits*, the large range of papers devoted to the movies and all more or less exploiting women's legs, the various trade papers, the women's story-papers (the *Oracle*, *Secrets*, *Peg's Paper*, etc. etc.), the needlework papers – these so numerous that a display of them alone will often fill an entire window – and in addition the long series of 'Yanks Mags' (*Fight Stories*, *Action Stories*, *Western Short Stories*, etc.), which are imported shop-soiled from America and sold at twopence-halfpenny or threepence. And the periodical proper shades off into the fourpenny novelette, the *Aldine Boxing Novels*, the *Boys' Friend Library*, the *School-girls' Own Library* and many others.

Probably the contents of these shops is the best available indication of what the mass of the English people really feels and thinks. Certainly nothing half so revealing exists in documentary form. Best-seller novels, for instance, tell one a great deal, but the novel is aimed almost exclusively at people above the £4-a-week level. The movies are probably a very unsafe guide to popular taste, because the film industry is virtually a monopoly, which means that it is not obliged to study its public at all closely. The same applies to some extent to the daily papers, and most of all to the radio. But it does not apply to the weekly paper with a smallish circulation and specialized subject-matter. Papers like the *Exchange and Mart*, for instance, or *Cage-Birds*, or the *Oracle*, or *Prediction*, or the *Matrimonial Times*, only exist because there is a definite demand for them, and they reflect the minds of their readers as a great national daily with a circulation of millions cannot possibly do.

Here I am only dealing with a single series of papers, the boys' twopenny weeklies, often inaccurately described as 'penny dreadfuls'. Falling strictly within this class there are at present ten papers, the *Gem*, *Magnet*, *Modern Boy*, *Triumph* and *Champion*, all owned by the Amalgamated Press, and the *Wizard*, *Rover*, *Skipper*, *Hotspur* and

Adventure, all owned by D. C. Thomson & Co. What the circulations of these papers are, I do not know. The editors and proprietors refuse to name any figures, and in any case the circulation of a paper carrying serial stories is bound to fluctuate widely. But there is no question that the combined public of the ten papers is a very large one. They are on sale in every town in England, and nearly every boy who reads at all goes through a phase of reading one or more of them. The *Gem* and *Magnet*, which are much the oldest of these papers, are of rather different type from the rest, and they have evidently lost some of their popularity during the past few years. A good many boys now regard them as old-fashioned and 'slow'. Nevertheless I want to discuss them first, because they are more interesting psychologically than the others, and also because the mere survival of such papers into the nineteen-thirties is a rather startling phenomenon.

The *Gem* and *Magnet* are sister-papers (characters out of one paper frequently appear in the other), and were both started more than thirty years ago. At that time, together with *Chums* and the old B[oys'] O[wn] P[aper], they were the leading players for boys, and they remained dominant till quite recently. Each of them carries every week a fifteen- or twenty-thousand-word school story, complete in itself, but usually more or less connected with the story of the week before. The *Gem* in addition to its school story carries one or more adventure serials. Otherwise the two papers are so much alike that they can be treated as one, though the *Magnet* has always been the better known of the two, probably because it possesses a really first-rate character in the fat boy, Billy Bunter.

The stories are stories of what purports to be public-school life, and the schools (Greyfriars in the *Magnet* and St Jim's in the *Gem*) are represented as ancient and fashionable foundations of the type of Eton or Winchester. All the leading characters are fourth-form boys aged fourteen or fifteen, older or younger boys only appearing in very minor parts. Like Sexton Blake and Nelson Lee, these boys continue week after week and year after year, never growing any older. Very occasionally a new boy arrives or a minor character drops out, but in at any rate the last twenty-five years the personnel has barely altered. All the principal characters in both papers – Bob Cherry, Tom Merry, Harry Wharton, Johnny Bull, Billy Bunter and the rest of them – were at Greyfriars or St Jim's long before the Great War, exactly the same age as at present, having much the same kind of adventures and talking almost exactly the same dialect. And not only the characters but the whole atmosphere of both the *Gem* and *Magnet* has been preserved unchanged, partly by means of very elaborate stylization. The stories in the *Magnet* are signed 'Frank Richards' and those in the *Gem* 'Martin Clifford', but a series lasting thirty years could hardly be the work of the same person every week.* Consequently they have to be written in a style that is easily imitated – an extraordinary, artificial, repeti-

---

* This is quite incorrect. These stories have been written throughout the whole period by 'Frank Richards' and 'Martin Clifford', who are one and the same person! See articles in *Horizon*, May 1940, and *Summer Pie*, summer 1944. [Author's footnote, 1945.]

tive style, quite different from anything else now existing in English literature. A couple of extracts will do as illustrations. Here is one from the *Magnet*:

> Groan!
> 'Shut up, Bunter!'
> Groan!

Shutting up was not really in Billy Bunter's line. He seldom shut up, though often requested to do so. On the present awful occasion the fat Owl of Greyfriars was less inclined than ever to shut up. And he did not shut up! He groaned, and groaned, and went on groaning.

Even groaning did not fully express Bunter's feeling. His feelings, in fact, were inexpressible.

There were six of them in the soup! Only one of the six uttered sounds of woe and lamentation. But that one, William George Bunter, uttered enough for the whole party and a little over.

Harry Wharton & Co. stood in a wrathy and worried group. They were landed and stranded, diddled, dished and done! etc. etc. etc.

Here is one from the *Gem*:

> 'Oh cwumbs!'
> 'Oh gum!'
> 'Oooogh!'
> 'Urrggh!'

Arthur Augustus sat up dizzily. He grabbed his handkerchief and pressed it to his damaged nose. Tom Merry sat up, gasping for breath. They looked at one another.

'Bai Jove! This is a go, deah boy!' gurgled Arthur Augustus.
'I have been thwown into a quite a fluttah! Oogh! The wottahs!
The wuffians! The fearful outsidahs! Wow!' etc. etc. etc.

Both of these extracts are entirely typical; you would
find something like them in almost every chapter of
every number, today or twenty-five years ago. The first
thing that anyone would notice is the extraordinary
amount of tautology (the first of these two passages
contains a hundred and twenty-five words and could be
compressed into about thirty), seemingly designed to
spin out the story, but actually playing its part in creating
the atmosphere. For the same reason various facetious
expressions are repeated over and over again; 'wrathy',
for instance, is a great favourite, and so is 'diddled, dished
and done'. 'Oooogh!' 'Grooo!' and 'Yaroo!' (stylized cries
of pain) recur constantly, and so does 'Ha! ha! ha!',
always given a line to itself, so that sometimes a quarter
of a column or thereabouts consists of 'Ha! ha! ha!'
The slang ('Go and eat coke!', 'What the thump!', 'You
frabjous ass!', etc. etc.) has never been altered, so that
the boys are now using slang which is at least thirty
years out of date. In addition, the various nicknames are
rubbed in on every possible occasion. Every few lines
we are reminded that Harry Wharton & Co. are 'the
Famous Five', Bunter is always 'the fat Owl' or 'the Owl
of the Remove', Vernon-Smith is always 'the Bounder
of Greyfriars', Gussy (the Honourable Arthur Augustus
D'Arcy) is always 'the swell of St Jim's', and so on and
so forth. There is a constant, untiring effort to keep the
atmosphere intact and to make sure that every new

reader learns immediately who is who. The result has been to make Greyfriars and St Jim's into an extraordinary little world of their own, a world which cannot be taken seriously by anyone over fifteen, but which at any rate is not easily forgotten. By a debasement of the Dickens technique a series of stereotyped 'characters' has been built up, in several cases very successfully. Billy Bunter, for instance, must be one of the best-known figures in English fiction; for the mere number of people who know him he ranks with Sexton Blake, Tarzan, Sherlock Holmes and a handful of characters in Dickens.

Needless to say, these stories are fantastically unlike life at a real public school. They run in cycles of rather differing types, but in general they are the clean-fun, knockabout type of story, with interest centring round horseplay, practical jokes, ragging masters, fights, canings, football, cricket and food. A constantly recurring story is one in which a boy is accused of some misdeed committed by another and is too much of a sportsman to reveal the truth. The 'good' boys are 'good' in the clean-living Englishman tradition – they keep in hard training, wash behind their ears, never hit below the belt, etc. etc. – and by way of contrast there is a series of 'bad' boys, Racke, Crooke, Loder and others, whose badness consists in betting, smoking cigarettes and frequenting public houses. All these boys are constantly on the verge of expulsion, but as it would mean a change of personnel if any boy were actually expelled, no one is ever caught out in any really serious offence. Stealing, for instance, barely enters as a motif. Sex is completely taboo, especially in the form in which it actually arises at public schools. Occasionally girls enter into the stories, and very rarely there is something approaching a mild flirtation, but it is always entirely in the spirit of clean fun. A boy and a girl enjoy going for bicycle rides together – that is all it ever amounts to. Kissing, for instance, would be regarded as 'soppy'. Even the bad boys are presumed to be completely sexless. When the *Gem* and *Magnet* were started, it is probable that there was a deliberate intention to get away from the guilty sex-ridden atmosphere that pervaded so much of the earlier literature for boys. In the nineties the *Boys' Own Paper*, for instance, used to have its correspondence columns full of terrifying warnings against masturbation, and books like *St Winifred's* and *Tom Brown's Schooldays* were heavy with homosexual feeling, though no doubt the authors were not fully aware of it. In the *Gem* and *Magnet* sex simply does not exist as a problem. Religion is also taboo; in the whole thirty years' issue of the two papers the word 'God' probably does not occur, except in 'God save the King'. On the other hand, there has always been a very strong 'temperance' strain. Drinking and, by association, smoking are regarded as rather disgraceful even in an adult ('shady' is the usual word), but at the same time as something irresistibly fascinating, a sort of substitute for sex. In their moral atmosphere the *Gem* and *Magnet* have a great deal in common with the Boy Scout movement, which started at about the same time.

All literature of this kind is partly plagiarism. Sexton Blake, for instance, started off quite frankly as an imitation of Sherlock Holmes, and still resembles him fairly strongly; he has hawk-like features, lives in Baker Street, smokes enormously and puts on a dressing-gown when he wants to think. The *Gem* and *Magnet* probably owe something to the school story writers who were flourishing when they began, Gunby Hadath, Desmond Coke and the rest, but they owe more to nineteenth-century models. In so far as Greyfriars and St Jim's are like real schools at all, they are much more like Tom Brown's Rugby than a modern public school. Neither school has an O.T.C. for instance, games are not compulsory, and the boys are even allowed to wear what clothes they like. But without doubt the main origin of these papers is *Stalky & Co*. This book has had an immense influence on boys' literature, and it is one of those books which have a sort of traditional reputation among people who have never even seen a copy of it. More than once in boys' weekly papers I have come across a reference to *Stalky & Co.* in which the word was spelt 'Storky'. Even the name of the chief comic among the Greyfriars masters, Mr Prout, is taken from *Stalky & Co.* and so is much of the slang: 'jape', 'merry', 'giddy', 'bizney' (business), 'frabjous', 'don't' for 'doesn't' – all of them out of date even when *Gem* and *Magnet* started. There are also traces of earlier origins. The name 'Greyfriars' is probably taken from Thackeray, and Gosling, the school porter in the *Magnet*, talks in an imitation of Dickens's dialect.

With all this, the supposed 'glamour' of public-school life is played for all it is worth. There is all the usual paraphernalia – lock-up, roll-call, house matches, fagging, prefects, cosy teas round the study fire, etc. etc. – and constant reference to the 'old school', the 'old grey stones' (both schools were founded in the early sixteenth century), the 'team spirit' of the 'Greyfriars men'. As for the snob-appeal, it is completely shameless. Each school has a titled boy or two whose titles are constantly thrust in the reader's face; other boys have the names of well-known aristocratic families, Talbot, Manners, Lowther. We are for ever being reminded that Gussy is the Honourable Arthur A. D'Arcy, son of Lord Eastwood, that Jack Blake is heir to 'broad acres', that Hurree Jamset Ram Singh (nicknamed Inky) is the Nabob of Bhanipur, that Vernon-Smith's father is a millionaire. Till recently the illustrations in both papers always depicted the boys in clothes imitated from those of Eton; in the last few years Greyfriars has changed over to blazers and flannel trousers, but St Jim's still sticks to the Eton jacket, and Gussy sticks to his top-hat. In the school magazine which appears every week as part of the *Magnet*, Harry Wharton writes an article discussing the pocket-money received by the 'fellows in the Remove', and reveals that some of them get as much as five pounds a week! This kind of thing is a perfectly deliberate incitement to wealth-fantasy. And here it is worth noticing a rather curious fact, and that is that the school story is a thing peculiar to England. So far as I know, there are extremely few school stories in foreign languages. The reason, obviously, is that in England education is mainly a matter of status. The most definite dividing line between the petite bourgeoisie and the working class is that the former pay for their education, and within the bourgeoisie there is another unbridgeable gulf between the 'public' school and the 'private' school. It is quite clear that there are tens and scores of thousands of people to whom every detail of life at a 'posh' public school is wildly thrilling and romantic. They happen to be outside that mystic world of quadrangles and house-colours, but they yearn after it, day-dream about it, live mentally in it for hours at a stretch. The question is, Who are these people? Who reads the *Gem* and *Magnet*?

Obviously one can never be quite certain about this kind of thing. All I can say from my own observation is this. Boys who are likely to go to public schools themselves generally read the *Gem* and *Magnet*, but they nearly always stop reading them when they are about twelve; they may continue for another year from force of habit, but by that time they have ceased to take them seriously. On the other hand, the boys at very cheap private schools, the schools that are designed for people who can't afford a public school but consider the council schools 'common', continue reading the *Gem* and *Magnet* for several years longer. A few years ago I was a teacher at two of these schools myself. I found that not only did virtually all the boys read the *Gem* and *Magnet*, but that they were still taking them fairly seriously when they were fifteen or even sixteen. These boys were the sons of shopkeepers, office employees and small business and professional men, and obviously it is this class that the *Gem* and *Magnet* are aimed at. But they are certainly read by working-class boys as well. They are generally on sale in the poorest quarters of big towns, and I have known them to be read by boys whom one might expect to be completely immune from public-school 'glamour'. I have seen a young coal miner, for instance, a lad who had already worked a year or two underground, eagerly reading the *Gem*. Recently I offered a batch of English papers to some British legionaries of the French Foreign Legion in North Africa; they picked out the *Gem* and *Magnet* first. Both papers are much read by girls,* and the Pen Pals' department of the *Gem* shows that it is read in every corner of the British Empire, by Australians, Canadians, Palestine Jews, Malays, Arabs, Straits Chinese, etc. etc. The editors evidently expect their readers to be aged round about fourteen, and the advertisements (milk chocolate, postage stamps, water pistols, blushing cured, home conjuring tricks, itching-powder, the Phine Phun Ring which runs a needle into your friend's hand, etc. etc.) indicate roughly the same age; there are also the Admiralty advertisements, however, which call for youths between seventeen and twenty-two. And there is no question that these papers are also read by adults. It is quite common for people to write to the editor and say that they have read every number of the *Gem* or *Magnet* for the past thirty years. Here, for instance, is a letter from a lady in Salisbury:

I can say of your splendid yarns of Harry Wharton & Co. of Greyfriars, that they never fail to reach a high standard. Without doubt they are the finest stories of their type on the market today, which is saying a good deal. They seem to bring you face to face with Nature. I have taken the *Magnet* from the

* There are several corresponding girls' papers. The *Schoolgirl* is companion-paper to the *Magnet* and has stories by 'Hilda Richards'. The characters are interchangeable to some extent. Bessie Bunter, Billy Bunter's sister, figures in the *Schoolgirl*. [Author's footnote.]

start, and have followed the adventures of Harry Wharton & Co. with rapt interest. I have no sons, but two daughters, and there's always a rush to be the first to read the grand old paper. My husband, too, was a staunch reader of the *Magnet* until he was suddenly taken away from us.

It is well worth getting hold of some copies of the *Gem* and *Magnet*, especially the *Gem*, simply to have a look at the correspondence columns. What is truly startling is the intense interest with which the pettiest details of life at Greyfriars and St Jim's are followed up. Here, for instance, are a few of the questions sent in by readers:

'What age is Dick Roylance?' 'How old is St Jim's?' 'Can you give me a list of the Shell and their studies?' 'How much did D'Arcy's monocle cost?' 'How is it fellows like Crooke are in the Shell and decent fellows like yourself are only in the Fourth?' 'What are the Form captain's three chief duties?' 'Who is the chemistry master at St Jim's?' (From a girl) 'Where is St Jim's situated? *Could* you tell me how to get there, as I would love to see the building? Are you boys just "phoneys", as I think you are?'

It is clear that many of the boys and girls who write these letters are living a complete fantasy-life. Sometimes a boy will write, for instance, give his age, height, weight, chest and biceps measurements and asking which member of the Shell or Fourth Form he most exactly resembles. The demand for a list of the studies on the Shell passage, with an exact account of who lives in each, is a very common one. The editors, of course, do everything in their power to keep up the illusion. In the *Gem* Jack Blake is supposed to write the answers to correspondents, and in the *Magnet* a couple of pages are always given up to the school magazine (the *Greyfriars Herald*, edited by Harry Wharton), and there is another page in which one or other character is written up each week. The stories run in cycles, two or three characters being kept in the foreground for several weeks at a time. First there will be a series of rollicking adventure stories, featuring the Famous Five and Billy Bunter; then a run of stories turning on mistaken identity, with Wibley (the make-up wizard) in the star part; then a run of more serious stories in which Vernon-Smith is trembling on the verge of expulsion. And here one comes upon the real secret of the *Gem* and *Magnet* and the probable reason why they continue to be read in spite of their obvious out-of-dateness.

It is that the characters are so carefully graded as to give almost every type of reader a character he can identify himself with. Most boys' papers aim at doing this, hence the boy-assistant (Sexton Blake's Tinker, Nelson Lee's Nipper, etc.) who usually accompanies the explorer, detective or what-not on his adventures. But in these cases there is only one boy, and usually it is much the same type of boy. In the *Gem* and *Magnet* there is a model for nearly everybody. There is the normal, athletic, high-spirited boy (Tom Merry, Jack Blake, Frank Nugent), a slightly rowdier version of this type (Bob Cherry), a more aristocratic version (Talbot, Manners), a quieter, more serious version (Harry Wharton), and a stolid, 'bulldog' version (Johnny Bull). Then there is the reckless, dare-devil type of boy (Vernon-Smith), the definitely 'clever', studious boy (Mark Linley, Dick Penfold), and the eccentric boy who is not good at games but possesses some special talent (Skinner, Wibley). And there is the scholarship-boy (Tom Redwing), an important figure in this class of story because he makes it possible for boys from very poor homes to project themselves into the public-school atmosphere. In addition there are Australian, Irish, Welsh, Manx, Yorkshire and Lancashire boys to play upon local patriotism. But the subtlety of characterization goes deeper than this. If one studies the correspondence columns one sees that there is probably *no* character in the *Gem* and *Magnet* whom some or other reader does not identify with, except the out-and-out comics, Coker, Billy Bunter, Fisher T. Fish (the money-grubbing American boy) and, of course, the masters. Bunter, though in his origin he probably owed something to the fat boy in *Pickwick*, is a real creation. His tight trousers against which boots and canes are constantly thudding, his astuteness in search of food, his postal order which never turns up, have made him famous wherever the Union Jack waves. But he is not a subject for day-dreams. On the other hand, another seeming figure of fun, Gussy (the Honourable Arthur A. D'Arcy, 'the swell of St Jim's'), is evidently much admired. Like everything else in the *Gem* and *Magnet*, Gussy is at least thirty years out of date. He is the 'knut' of the early twentieth century or even the 'masher' of the nineties ('Bai Jove, deah boy!' and 'Weally, I shall be obliged to give you a feahful thwashin!'), the monocled idiot who made good on the fields of Mons and Le

Cateau. And his evident popularity goes to show how deep the snob-appeal of this type is. English people are extremely fond of the titled ass (cf. Lord Peter Wimsey) who always turns up trumps in the moment of emergency. Here is a letter from one of Gussy's girl admirers:

I think you're too hard on Gussy. I wonder he's still in existence, the way you treat him. He's my hero. Did you know I write lyrics? How's this – to the tune of 'Goody Goody'?

> Gonna get my gas-mask, join the A.R.P.
> 'Cos I'm wise to all those bombs you drop on me.
> > Gonna dig myself a trench
> > Inside the garden fence;
> > Gonna seal my windows up with tin
> > So that the tear gas can't get in;
> Gonna park my cannon right outside the kerb
> With a note to Adolf Hitler: 'Don't disturb!'
> > And if I never fall in Nazi hands
> > That's soon enough for me
> > Gonna get my gas-mask, join the A.R.P.

P.S. – Do you get on well with girls?

I quote this in full because (dated April 1939) it is interesting as being probably the earliest mention of Hitler in the *Gem*. In the *Gem* there is also a heroic fat boy, Fatty Wynn, as a set-off against Bunter. Vernon-Smith, 'the Bounder of the Remove', a Byronic character, always on the verge of the sack, is another great favourite. And even some of the cads probably have their following. Loder, for instance, 'the rotter of the Sixth', is a cad, but he is also a highbrow and given to saying sarcastic things about football and the team spirit. The boys of the Remove only think him all the more of a cad for this, but a certain type of boy would probably identify with him. Even Racke, Crooke and Co. are probably admired by small boys who think it diabolically wicked to smoke cigarettes. (A frequent question in the correspondence column: 'What brand of cigarettes does Racke smoke?')

Naturally the politics of the *Gem* and *Magnet* are Conservative, but in a completely pre-1914 style, with no Fascist tinge. In reality their basic political assumptions are two: nothing ever changes, and foreigners are funny. In the *Gem* of 1939 Frenchmen are still Froggies and Italians are still Dagoes. Mossoo, the French master at Greyfriars, is the usual comic-paper Frog, with pointed beard, pegtop trousers, etc. Inky, the Indian boy, though a rajah, and therefore possessing snob-appeal, is also the comic babu of the *Punch* tradition. ('The rowfulness is not the proper caper, my esteemed Bob,' said Inky. 'Let dogs delight in the barkfulness and bitefulness, but the soft answer is the cracked pitcher that goes longest to a bird in the bush, as the English proverb remarks.') Fisher T. Fish is the old-style stage Yankee ('Waal, I guess,' etc.) dating from a period of Anglo-American jealousy. Wun Lung, the Chinese boy (he has rather faded out of late, no doubt because some of the *Magnet*'s readers are Straits Chinese), is the nineteenth-century pantomime Chinaman, with saucershaped hat, pigtail and pidgin-English. The assumption all along is not only that foreigners are comics who are put there for us to laugh at, but that they can be classified in much the same way as insects. That is why in all boys' papers, not only the *Gem* and *Magnet*, a Chinese is invariably portrayed with a pigtail. It is the thing you recognize him by, like the Frenchman's beard or the Italian's barrel-organ. In papers of this kind it occasionally happens that when the setting of a story is in a foreign country some attempt is made to describe the natives as individual human beings, but as a rule it is assumed that foreigners of any one race are all alike and will conform more or less exactly to the following patterns:

FRENCHMAN: Excitable. Wears beard, gesticulates wildly.

SPANIARD, MEXICAN ETC.: Sinister, treacherous.

ARAB, AFGHAN ETC.: Sinister, treacherous.

CHINESE: Sinister, treacherous, wears pigtails.

ITALIAN: Excitable. Grinds barrel-organ or carries stiletto.

SWEDE, DANE ETC.: Kind-hearted, stupid.

NEGRO: Comic, very faithful.

The working classes only enter into the *Gem* and *Magnet* as comics or semi-villains (race-course touts etc.). As for class-friction, trade unionism, strikes, slumps, unemployment, Fascism and civil war – not a mention. Somewhere or other in the thirty years' issue of the two papers you might perhaps find the word 'Socialism', but you would have to look a long time for it. If the Russian Revolution is anywhere referred to, it will be indirectly, in the word 'Bolshy' (meaning a person of violent disagreeable habits). Hitler and the Nazis are just beginning to make their appearance, in the sort of reference I quoted above. The war crisis of September 1938 made just enough impression to produce a story in which Mr Vernon-Smith, the Bounder's millionaire father, cashed in on the general panic by buying up country houses in order to sell them to 'crisis scuttlers'. But that is probably as near to noticing the European situation as the *Gem* and *Magnet* will come, until the war actually starts.* That does not mean these papers are unpatriotic – quite the contrary! Throughout the Great War the *Gem* and *Magnet* were perhaps the most consistently and cheerfully patriotic papers in England. Almost every week the boys caught a spy or pushed a conchy into the army, and during the rationing period 'EAT LESS BREAD' was printed in large type on every page. But their patriotism has nothing whatever to do with power politics or 'ideological' warfare. It is more akin to family loyalty, and actually it gives one a valuable clue to the attitude of ordinary people, especially the huge untouchable block of the middle class and the better-off working class. These people are patriotic to the middle of their bones, but they do not feel that what happens in foreign countries is any of their business. When England is in danger they rally to its defence as a matter of course, but in between times they are not interested. After all, England is always in the right and England always wins, so why worry? It is an attitude that has been shaken during the past twenty years, but not so deeply as is sometimes supposed.

* This was written some months before the outbreak of war. Up to the end of September 1939 no mention of the war has appeared in either paper. [Author's footnote.]

Failure to understand it is one of the reasons why left-wing political parties are seldom able to produce an acceptable foreign policy.

The mental world of the *Gem* and *Magnet*, therefore, is something like this:

The year is 1910 – or 1940, but it is all the same. You are at Greyfriars, a rosy-cheeked boy of fourteen in posh, tailor-made clothes, sitting down to tea in your study on the Remove passage after an exciting game of football which was won by an odd goal in the last half-minute. There is a cosy fire in the study, and outside the wind is whistling. The ivy clusters thickly round the old grey stones. The King is on his throne and the pound is worth a pound. Over in Europe the comic foreigners are jabbering and gesticulating, but the grim grey battleships of the British Fleet are steaming up the Channel and at the outposts of Empire the monocled Englishmen are holding the niggers at bay. Lord Mauleverer has just got another fiver and we are all settling down to a tremendous tea of sausages, sardines, crumpets, potted meat, jam and doughnuts. After tea we shall sit round the study fire having a good laugh at Billy Bunter and discussing the team for next week's match against Rookwood. Everything is safe, solid and unquestionable. Everything will be the same for ever and ever. That approximately is the atmosphere.

But now turn from the *Gem* and *Magnet* to the more up-to-date papers which have appeared since the Great War. The truly significant thing is that they have more points of resemblance to the *Gem* and *Magnet* than points of difference. But it is better to consider the differences first.

There are eight of these newer papers, the *Modern Boy*, *Triumph*, *Champion*, *Wizard*, *Rover*, *Skipper*, *Hotspur* and *Adventure*. All of these have appeared since the Great War, but except for the *Modern Boy* none of them is less than five years old. Two papers which ought also to be mentioned briefly here, though they are not strictly in the same class as the rest, are the *Detective Weekly* and the *Thriller*, both owned by the Amalgamated Press. The *Detective Weekly* has taken over Sexton Blake. Both of these papers admit a certain amount of sex-interest into their stories, and though certainly read by boys, they are not aimed at them exclusively. All the others are boys' papers pure and simple, and they are sufficiently alike to be considered together. There does not seem to be any notable difference between Thomson's publications and those of the Amalgamated Press.

As soon as one looks at these papers one sees their technical superiority to the *Gem* and *Magnet*. To begin with, they have the great advantage of not being written entirely by one person. Instead of one long complete story, a number of the *Wizard* or *Hotspur* consists of half a dozen or more serials, none of which goes on for ever. Consequently there is far more variety and far less padding, and none of the tiresome stylization and facetiousness of the *Gem* and *Magnet*. Look at these two extracts, for example:

Billy Bunter groaned.

A quarter of an hour had elapsed out of the two hours that Bunter was booked for extra French.

In a quarter of an hour there were only fifteen minutes!

But every one of those minutes seemed inordinately long to Bunter. They seemed to crawl by like tired snails.

Looking at the clock in Class-room No. 10 the fat Owl could hardly believe that only fifteen minutes had passed. It seemed more like fifteen hours, if not fifteen days!

Other fellows were in extra French as well as Bunter. They did not matter. Bunter did! (*Magnet.*)

After a terrible climb, hacking out handholds in the smooth ice every step of the way up, Sergeant Lionheart Logan of the Mounties was now clinging like a human fly to the face of an icy cliff, as smooth and treacherous as a giant pane of glass.

An Arctic blizzard, in all its fury, was buffeting his body, driving the blinding snow into his face, seeking to tear his fingers loose from their handholds and dash him to death on the jagged boulders which lay at the foot of the cliff a hundred feet below.

Crouching among those boulders were eleven villainous trappers who had done their best to shoot down Lionheart and his companion, Constable Jim Rogers – until the blizzard had blotted the two Mounties out of sight from below. (*Wizard.*)

The second extract gets you some distance with the story, the first takes a hundred words to tell you that Bunter is in the detention class. Moreover, by not concentrating on school stories (in point of numbers the school story slightly predominates in all these papers, except the *Thriller* and *Detective Weekly*), the *Wizard*, *Hotspur*, etc. have far greater opportunities for sensationalism. Merely looking at the cover illustrations of the papers which I have on the table in front of me, here are some of the things I see. On one a cowboy is clinging by his toes to the wing of an aeroplane in mid-air and shooting down another aeroplane with his revolver. On another a Chinese is swimming for his life down a sewer with a swarm of ravenous-looking rats swimming after him. On another an engineer is lighting a stick of dynamite while a steel robot feels for him with its claws. On another a man in airman's costume is fighting bare-handed against a rat somewhat larger than a donkey. On another a nearly naked man of terrific muscular development has just seized a lion by the tail and flung it thirty yards over the wall of an arena, with the words, 'Take back your blooming lion!' Clearly no school story can compete with this kind of thing. From time to time the school buildings may catch fire or the French master may turn out to be the head of an international anarchist gang, but in a general way the interest must centre round cricket, school rivalries, practical jokes, etc. There is not much room for bombs, death-rays, sub-machine-guns, aeroplanes, mustangs, octopuses, grizzly bears or gangsters.

Examination of a large number of these papers shows that, putting aside school stories, the favourite subjects are Wild West, Frozen North, Foreign Legion, crime (always from the detective's angle), the Great War (Air Force or Secret Service, not the infantry), the Tarzan motif in varying forms, professional football, tropical exploration, historical romance (Robin Hood, Cavaliers and Roundheads, etc.) and scientific invention. The Wild West still leads, at any rate as a setting, though the Red Indian seems to be fading out. The one theme that is really new is the scientific one. Death-rays, Martians, invisible men, robots, helicopters and interplanetary rockets figure largely; here and there there are even far-off rumours of psychotherapy and ductless glands. Whereas the *Gem* and *Magnet* derive from Dickens and Kipling, the *Wizard, Champion, Modern Boy*, etc. owe a great deal to H. G. Wells, who, rather than Jules Verne, is the father of 'Scientifiction'. Naturally, it is the magical, Martian aspect of science that is most exploited, but one or two papers include serious articles on scientific subjects, besides quantities of informative snippets. (Examples: 'A Kauri tree in Queensland, Australia, is over 12,000 years old'; 'Nearly 50,000 thunderstorms occur every day'; 'Helium gas costs £1 per 1,000 cubic feet'; 'There are over 500 varieties of spiders in Great Britain'; 'London firemen use 14,000,000 gallons of water annually', etc. etc.) There is a marked advance in intellectual curiosity and, on the whole, in the demand made on the reader's attention. In practice the *Gem* and *Magnet* and the post-war papers are read by much the same public, but the mental age aimed at seems to have risen by a year or two years – an improvement probably corresponding to the improvement in elementary education since 1909.

The other thing that has emerged in the post-war boys' papers, though not to anything like the extent one would expect, is bully-worship and the cult of violence.

If one compares the *Gem* and *Magnet* with a genuinely modern paper, the thing that immediately strikes one is the absence of the leader-principle. There is no central dominating character; instead there are fifteen or twenty characters, all more or less on an equality, with whom readers of different types can identify. In the more modern papers this is not usually the case. Instead of identifying with a schoolboy of more or less his own age, the reader of the *Skipper*, *Hotspur*, etc. is led to identify with a G-man, with a Foreign Legionary, with some variant of Tarzan, with an air ace, a master spy, an explorer, a pugilist – at any rate with some single all-powerful character who dominates everyone about him and whose usual method of solving any problem is a sock on the jaw. This character is intended as a super-man, and as physical strength is the form of power that boys can best understand, he is usually a sort of human gorilla; in the Tarzan type of story he is sometimes actually a giant, eight or ten feet high. At the same time the scenes of violence in nearly all these stories are remarkably harmless and unconvincing. There is a great difference in tone between even the most bloodthirsty English paper and the threepenny Yank Mags, *Fight Stories*, *Action Stories*, etc. (not strictly boys' papers, but largely read by boys). In the Yank Mags you get real blood-lust, really gory descriptions of the all-in, jump-on-his-testicles style of fighting, written in a jargon that has been perfected by people who brood endlessly on violence. A paper like *Fight Stories*, for instance, would have very little appeal except to sadists and masochists. You can see the comparative gentleness of English civilization by the amateurish way in which prize-fighting is always described in the boys' weeklies. There is no specialized vocabulary. Look at these four extracts, two English, two American:

When the gong sounded, both men were breathing heavily, and each had great red marks on his chest, Bill's chin was bleeding, and Ben had a cut over his right eye.

Into their corners they sank, but when the gong clanged again they were up swiftly, and they went like tigers at each other. (*Rover.*)

He walked in stolidly and smashed a clublike right to my face. Blood spattered and I went back on my heels, but surged in and ripped my right under his heart. Another right smashed full on Sven's already battered mouth, and, spitting out the fragments of a tooth, he crashed a flailing left to my body. (*Fight Stories.*)

It was amazing to watch the black Panther at work. His muscles rippled and slid under his dark skin. There was all the power and grace of a giant cat in his swift and terrible onslaught.

He volleyed blows with a bewildering speed for so huge a fellow. In a moment Ben was simply blocking with his gloves as well as he could. Ben was really a past-master of defence. He had many fine victories behind him. But the Negro's rights and lefts crashed through openings that hardly any other fighter could have found. (*Wizard.*)

Haymakers which packed the bludgeoning weight of forest monarchs crashing down under the ax hurled into the bodies of the two heavies as they swapped punches. (*Fight Stories.*)

Notice how much more knowledgeable the American extracts sound. They are written for devotees of the

prize-ring, the others are not. Also, it ought to be empha-
sized that on its level the moral code of the English boys'
papers is a decent one. Crime and dishonesty are never
held up to admiration, there is none of the cynicism and
corruption of the American gangster story. The huge
sale of the Yank Mags in England shows that there is a
demand for that kind of thing, but very few English
writers seem able to produce it. When hatred of Hitler
became a major emotion in America, it was interesting
to see how promptly 'anti-Fascism' was adapted to
pornographic purposes by the editors of the Yank Mags.
One magazine which I have in front of me is given up
to a long, complete story, 'When Hell Came to America',
in which the agents of a 'blood-maddened European
dictator' are trying to conquer the U.S.A. with death-rays
and invisible aeroplanes. There is the frankest appeal to
sadism, scenes in which the Nazis tie bombs to women's
backs and fling them off heights to watch them blown
to pieces in mid-air, others in which they tie naked girls
together by their hair and prod them with knives to make
them dance, etc. etc. The editor comments solemnly on
all this, and uses it as a plea for tightening up restrictions
against immigrants. On another page of the same paper:
'LIVES OF THE HOTCHA CHORUS GIRLS. Reveals all the
intimate secrets and fascinating pastimes of the famous
Broadway Hotcha girls. NOTHING IS OMITTED. Price
10C.' 'HOW TO LOVE. 10C.' 'FRENCH PHOTO RING, 25C.'
'NAUGHTY NUDIES TRANSFERS. From the outside of the
glass you see a beautiful girl, innocently dressed. Turn
it around and look through the glass and oh! what a
difference! Set of 3 transfers 25C.' etc. etc. etc. There is

nothing at all like this in any English paper likely to be read by boys. But the process of Americanization is going on all the same. The American ideal, the 'he-man', the 'tough guy', the gorilla who puts everything right by socking everybody else on the jaw, now figures in probably a majority of boys' papers. In one serial now running in the *Skipper* he is always portrayed, ominously enough, swinging a rubber truncheon.

The development of the *Wizard*, *Hotspur*, etc., as against the earlier boys' papers, boils down to this: better technique, more scientific interest, more bloodshed, more leader-worship. But, after all, it is the *lack* of development that is the really striking thing.

To begin with, there is no political development whatever. The world of the *Skipper* and the *Champion* is still the pre-1914 world of the *Magnet* and the *Gem*. The Wild West story, for instance, with its cattle-rustlers, lynch-law and other paraphernalia belonging to the eighties, is a curiously archaic thing. It is worth noticing that in papers of this type it is always taken for granted that adventures only happen at the ends of the earth, in tropical forests, in Arctic wastes, in African deserts, on Western prairies, in Chinese opium dens – everywhere, in fact, except the place where things really *do* happen. That is a belief dating from thirty or forty years ago, when the new continents were in process of being opened up. Nowadays, of course, if you really want adventure, the place to look for it is in Europe. But apart from the picturesque side of the Great War, contemporary history is carefully excluded. And except that Americans are now admired instead of being laughed at, foreigners are exactly the same figures of fun that they always were. If a Chinese character appears, he is still the sinister pigtailed opium-smuggler of Sax Rohmer; no indication that things have been happening in China since 1912 – no indication that a war is going on there, for instance. If a Spaniard appears, he is still a 'dago' or a 'greaser' who rolls cigarettes and stabs people in the back; no indication that things have been happening in Spain. Hitler and the Nazis have not yet appeared, or are barely making their appearance. There will be plenty about them in a little while, but it will be from a strictly patriotic angle (Britain versus Germany), with the real meaning of the struggle kept out of sight as much as possible. As for the Russian Revolution, it is extremely difficult to find any reference to it in any of these papers. When Russia is mentioned at all it is usually in an information snippet (example: 'There are 29,000 centenarians in the U.S.S.R.'), and any reference to the Revolution is indirect and twenty years out of date. In one story in the *Rover*, for instance, somebody has a tame bear, and as it is a Russian bear, it is nicknamed Trotsky – obviously an echo of the 1917–23 period and not of recent controversies. The clock has stopped at 1910. Britannia rules the waves, and no one has heard of slumps, booms, unemployment, dictatorships, purges or concentration camps.

And in social outlook there is hardly any advance. The snobbishness is somewhat less open than in the *Gem* and *Magnet* – that is the most one can possibly say. To begin with, the school story, always partly dependent on snob-appeal, is by no means eliminated. Every number of a boys' paper includes at least one school story, these stories slightly outnumbering the Wild Westerns. The very elaborate fantasy-life of the *Gem* and *Magnet* is not imitated and there is more emphasis on extraneous adventure, but the social atmosphere (old grey stones) is much the same. When a new school is introduced at the beginning of a story we are often told in just about those words that 'it was a very posh school'. From time to time a story appears which is ostensibly directed *against* snobbery. The scholarship-boy (cf. Tom Redwing in the *Magnet*) makes fairly frequent appearances, and what is essentially the same theme is sometimes presented in this form; there is great rivalry between two schools, one of which considers itself more 'posh' than the other, and there are fights, practical jokes, football matches, etc. always ending in the discomfiture of the snobs. If one glances very superficially at some of these stories it is possible to imagine that a democratic spirit has crept into the boys' weeklies, but when one looks more closely one sees that they merely reflected the bitter jealousies that exist within the white-collar class. Their real function is to allow the boy who goes to a cheap private school (*not* a Council school) to feel that his school is just as 'posh' in the sight of God as Winchester or Eton. The sentiment of school loyalty ('We're better than the fellows down the road'), a thing almost unknown to the real working class, is still kept up. As these stories are written by many different hands, they do, of course, vary a good deal in tone. Some are reasonably free from snobbishness, in others money and pedigree are exploited even more shamelessly than in the

Gem and *Magnet*. In one that I came across an actual *majority* of the boys mentioned were titled.

Where working-class characters appear, it is usually either as comics (jokes about tramps, convicts, etc.) or as prize-fighters, acrobats, cowboys, professional foot-ballers and Foreign Legionaries – in other words, as adventurers. There is no facing of the facts about work-ing-class life, or, indeed, about *working* life of any descrip-tion. Very occasionally one may come across a realistic description of, say, work in a coal mine, but in all probability it will only be there as the background of some lurid adventure. In any case the central character is not likely to be a coal-miner. Nearly all the time the boy who reads these papers – in nine cases out of ten a boy who is going to spend his life working in a shop, in a factory or in some subordinate job in an office – is led to identify with people in positions of command, above all with people who are never troubled by shortage of money. The Lord Peter Wimsey figure, the seeming idiot who drawls and wears a monocle but is always to the fore in moments of danger, turns up over and over again. (This character is a great favourite in Secret Service stories.) And, as usual, the heroic characters all have to talk B.B.C.; they may talk Scottish or Irish or American, but no one in a star part is ever permitted to drop an aitch. Here it is worth comparing the social atmosphere of the boys' weeklies with that of the women's weeklies, the *Oracle*, the *Family Star*, *Peg's Paper*, etc.

The women's papers are aimed at an older public and are read for the most part by girls who are working for a living. Consequently they are on the surface much more realistic. It is taken for granted, for example, that nearly everyone has to live in a big town and work at a more or less dull job. Sex, so far from being taboo, is *the* subject. The short, complete stories, the special feature of these papers, are generally of the 'came the dawn' type: the heroine narrowly escapes losing her 'boy' to a designing rival, or the 'boy' loses his job and has to postpone marriage, but presently gets a better job. The changeling-fantasy (a girl brought up in a poor home is 'really' the child of rich parents) is another favourite. Where sensationalism comes in, usually in the serials, it arises out of the more domestic type of crime, such as bigamy, forgery or sometimes murder; no Martians, death-rays or international anarchist gangs. These papers are at any rate aiming at credibility, and they have a link with real life in their correspondence columns, where genuine problems are being discussed. Ruby M. Ayres's column of advice in the *Oracle*, for instance, is extremely sensible and well written. And yet the world of the *Oracle* and *Peg's Paper* is a pure fantasy-world. It is the same fantasy all the time, pretending to be richer than you are. The chief impression that one carries away from almost every story in these papers is of frightful, over-whelming 'refinement'. Ostensibly the characters are working-class people, but their habits, the interiors of their houses, their clothes, their outlook and, above all, their speech are entirely middle class. They are all living at several pounds a week above their income. And need-less to say, that is just the impression that is intended. The idea is to give the bored factory-girl or worn-out mother of five a dream-life in which she pictures herself – not actually as a duchess (that convention has gone out) but as, say, the wife of a bank-manager. Not only is a five-to-six-pound-a-week standard of life set up as the ideal, it is tacitly assumed that that is how working-class people really *do* live. The major facts are simply not faced. It is admitted, for instance, that people sometimes lose their jobs; but then the dark clouds roll away and they get better jobs instead. No mention of unemployment as sometimes permanent and inevitable, no mention of the dole, no mention of trade unionism. No suggestion anywhere that there can be anything wrong with the system *as a system*; there are only individual misfortunes, which are generally due to somebody's wickedness and can in any case be put right in the last chapter. Always the dark clouds roll away, the kind employer raises Alfred's wages, and there are jobs for everybody except the drunks. It is still the world of the *Wizard* and the *Gem*, except that there are orange-blossoms instead of machine-guns.

The outlook inculcated by all these papers is that of a rather exceptionally stupid member of the Navy League in the year 1910. Yes, it may be said, but what does it matter? And in any case, what else do you expect?

Of course no one in his senses would want to turn the so-called penny dreadful into a realistic novel or a Socialist tract. An adventure story must of its nature be more or less remote from real life. But, as I have tried to make clear, the unreality of the *Wizard* and the *Gem* is not so artless as it looks. These papers exist because of a specialized demand, because boys at certain ages find it necessary to read about Martians, death-rays, grizzly bears and gangsters. They get what they are looking for, but they get it wrapped up in the illusions which their future employers think suitable for them. To what extent people draw their ideas from fiction is disputable. Personally I believe that most people are influenced far more than they would care to admit by novels, serial stories, films and so forth, and that from this point of view the worst books are often the most important, because they are usually the ones that are read earliest in life. It is probable that many people who could consider themselves extemely sophisticated and 'advanced' are actually carrying through life an imaginative background which they acquired in childhood from (for instance) Sapper and Ian Hay. If that is so, the boys' twopenny weeklies are of the deepest importance. Here is the stuff that is read somewhere between the ages of twelve and eighteen by a very large proportion, perhaps an actual majority, of English boys, including many who will never read anything else except newspapers; and along with it they are absorbing a set of beliefs which would be regarded as hopelessly out of date in the Central Office of the Conservative Party. All the better because it is done indirectly, there is being pumped into them the conviction that the major problems of our time do not exist, that there is nothing wrong with *laissez-faire* capitalism, that foreigners are unimportant comics and that the British Empire is a sort of charity-concern which will last for ever. Considering who owns these papers, it is difficult to believe that this is unintentional. Of the twelve papers I have been discussing (i.e. twelve including the

Thriller and *Detective Weekly*) seven are the property of
the Amalgamated Press, which is one of the biggest
press-combines in the world and controls more than a
hundred different papers. The *Gem* and *Magnet*, therefore, are closely linked up with the *Daily Telegraph* and
the *Financial Times*. This in itself would be enough to
rouse certain suspicions, even if it were not obvious that
the stories in the boys' weeklies are politically vetted. So
it appears that if you feel the need of a fantasy-life in
which you travel to Mars and fight lions bare-handed
(and what boy doesn't?) you can only have it by de-
livering yourself over, mentally, to people like Lord
Camrose. For there is no competition. Throughout the
whole of this run of papers the differences are negligible,
and on this level no others exist. This raises the question,
why is there no such thing as a left-wing boys' paper?

At first glance such an idea merely makes one slightly
sick. It is so horribly easy to imagine what a left-wing
boys' paper would be like, if it existed. I remember
in 1920 or 1921 some optimistic person handing round
Communist tracts among a crowd of public-school boys.
The tract I received was of the question-and-answer kind:

Q. 'Can a Boy Communist be a Boy Scout, Comrade?'
A. 'No, Comrade.'
Q. 'Why, Comrade?'
A. 'Because, Comrade, a Boy Scout must salute the Union
Jack, which is the symbol of tyranny and oppression,' etc. etc.

Now, suppose that at this moment somebody started
a left-wing paper deliberately aimed at boys of twelve or

fourteen. I do not suggest that the whole of its contents would be exactly like the tract I have quoted above, but does anyone doubt that they would be *something* like it? Inevitably such a paper would either consist of dreary uplift or it would be under Communist influence and given over to adulation of Soviet Russia; in either case no normal boy would ever look at it. Highbrow literature apart, the whole of the existing left-wing press, in so far as it is at all vigorously 'left', is one long tract. The one Socialist paper in England which could live a week on its merits *as a paper* is the *Daily Herald*, and how much Socialism is there in the *Daily Herald*? At this moment, therefore, a paper with a 'left' slant and at the same time likely to have an appeal to ordinary boys in their teens is something almost beyond hoping for.

But it does not follow that it is impossible. There is no clear reason why every adventure story should necessarily be mixed up with snobbishness and gutter patriotism. For, after all, the stories in the *Hotspur* and the *Modern Boy* are not Conservative tracts; they are merely adventure stories with a Conservative bias. It is fairly easy to imagine the process being reversed. It is possible, for instance, to imagine a paper as thrilling and lively as the *Hotspur*, but with subject-matter and 'ideology' a little more up to date. It is even possible (though this raises other difficulties) to imagine a women's paper at the same literary level as the *Oracle*, dealing in approximately the same kind of story, but taking rather more account of the realities of working-class life. Such things have been done before, though not in England. In the last years of the Spanish monarchy there was a large output in Spain of left-wing novelettes, some of them evidently of Anarchist origin. Unfortunately at the time when they were appearing I did not see their social significance, and I lost the collection of them that I had, but no doubt copies would still be procurable. In get-up and style of story they were very similar to the English fourpenny novelette, except that their inspiration was 'left'. If, for instance, a story described police pursuing Anarchists through the mountains, it would be from the point of view of the Anarchists and not of the police. An example nearer to hand is the Soviet film *Chapayev*, which has been shown a number of times in London. Technically, by the standards of the time when it was made, *Chapayev* is a first-rate film, but mentally, in spite of the unfamiliar Russian background, it is not so very remote from Hollywood. The one thing that lifts it out of the ordinary is the remarkable performance by the actor who takes the part of the White officer (the fat one) – a performance which looks very like an inspired piece of gagging. Otherwise the atmosphere is familiar. All the usual paraphernalia is there – heroic fight against odds, escape at the last moment, shots of galloping horses, love interest, comic relief. The film is in fact a fairly ordinary one, except that its tendency is 'left'. In a Hollywood film of the Russian Civil War the Whites would probably be angels and the Reds demons. In the Russian version the Reds are angels and the Whites demons. That also is a lie, but, taking the long view, it is a less pernicious lie than the other.

Here several difficult problems present themselves. Their general nature is obvious enough, and I do not want to discuss them. I am merely pointing to the fact that, in England, popular imaginative literature is a field that left-wing thought has never begun to enter. *All* fiction from the novels in the mushroom libraries downwards is censored in the interests of the ruling class. And boys' fiction above all, the blood-and-thunder stuff which nearly every boy devours at some time or other, is sodden in the worst illusions of 1910. The fact is only unimportant if one believes that what is read in childhood leaves no impression behind. Lord Camrose and his colleagues evidently believe nothing of the kind, and, after all, Lord Camrose ought to know.

Women's Twopenny Papers

Some years ago, in the course of an article about boys' weekly papers, I made some passing remarks about women's papers – I mean the twopenny ones of the type of *Peg's Paper*, often called 'love books.' This brought me, among much other correspondence, a long letter from a woman who had contributed to and worked for the *Lucky Star*, the *Golden Star*, *Peg's Paper*, *Secrets*, the *Oracle*, and a number of kindred papers. Her main point was that I had been wrong in saying that these papers aim at creating wealth fantasy. Their stories are 'in no sense Cinderella stories' and do not exploit the 'she married her boss' motif. My correspondent adds:

Unemployment is mentioned – quite frequently . . . The dole and the trade union are certainly never mentioned. The latter may be influenced by the fact that the largest publishers of these women's magazines are a non-union house. One is never allowed to criticise the system, or to show up the class struggle for what it really is, and the word Socialist is *never* mentioned – all this is perfectly true. But it might be interesting to add that class feeling is not altogether absent. The rich are often shown as mean, and as cruel and crooked money-makers. The rich and idle beau is nearly always planning marriage without a ring, and the lass is rescued by her strong, hard-working garage hand. Men with cars are generally 'bad' and men in well-cut, expensive suits are nearly always crooks. The ideal of most of these stories is *not* an income worthy of a bank manager's wife, but a life that is 'good'. A life with an upright, kind husband, however poor, with babies and a 'little cottage'. The stories are conditioned to show that the meagre life is not so bad really, as you are at least honest and happy, and that riches bring trouble and false friends. The poor are given moral values to aspire to as something within their reach.

There are many comments I could make here, but I choose to take up the point of the moral superiority of the poor being combined with the non-mention of trade unions and Socialism. There is no doubt that this is deliberate policy. In one women's paper I actually read a story dealing with a strike in a coal-mine, and even in that connection trade unionism was not mentioned. When the U.S.S.R. entered the war one of these papers promptly cashed in with a serial entitled *Her Soviet Lover*, but we may be sure that Marxism did not enter into it very largely.

The fact is that this business about the moral superiority of the poor is one of the deadliest forms of escapism the ruling class have evolved. You may be downtrodden and swindled, but in the eyes of God you are superior to your oppressors, and by means of films and magazines you can enjoy a fantasy existence in which you constantly triumph over the people who defeat you in real life. In any form of art designed to appeal to large numbers of people, it is an almost unheard of thing for a rich man to get the better of a poor man. The rich man is usually 'bad', and his machinations are invariably frustrated.

'Good poor man defeats bad rich man' is an accepted formula, whereas if it were the other way about we should feel that there was something very wrong somewhere. This is as noticeable in films as in the cheap magazines, and it was perhaps most noticeable of all in the old silent films, which travelled from country to country and had to appeal to a very varied audience. The vast majority of the people who will see a film are poor, and so it is politic to make a poor man the hero. Film magnates, Press lords and the like amass quite a lot of their wealth by pointing out that wealth is wicked.

The formula 'good poor man defeats bad rich man' is simply a subtler version of 'pie in the sky'. It is a sublimation of the class struggle. So long as you can dream of yourself as a 'strong, hard-working garage hand' giving some moneyed crook a sock on the jaw, the *real* facts can be forgotten. That is a cleverer dodge than wealth fantasy. But, curiously enough, reality does enter into these women's magazines, not through the stories but through the correspondence columns, especially in those papers that give free medical advice. Here you can read harrowing tales of 'bad legs' and haemorrhoids, written by middle-aged women who give themselves such pseudonyms as 'A Sufferer', 'Mother of Nine', and 'Always Constipated'. To compare these letters with the love stories that lie cheek by jowl with them is to see how vast a part mere day-dreaming plays in modern life.

The Art of Donald McGill

Who does not know the 'comics' of the cheap stationers' windows, the penny or twopenny coloured postcards with their endless succession of fat women in tight bathing-dresses and their crude drawing and unbearable colours, chiefly hedge-sparrow's egg tint and Post Office red?

This question ought to be rhetorical, but it is a curious fact that many people seem to be unaware of the existence of these things, or else to have a vague notion that they are something to be found only at the seaside, like nigger minstrels or peppermint rock. Actually they are on sale everywhere – they can be bought at nearly any Woolworth's, for example – and they are evidently produced in enormous numbers, new series constantly appearing. They are not to be confused with the various other types of comic illustrated postcard, such as the sentimental ones dealing with puppies and kittens or the Wendyish, sub-pornographic ones which exploit the love-affairs of children. They are a genre of their own, specializing in very 'low' humour, the mother-in-law, baby's nappy, policemen's boots type of joke, and distinguishable from all the other kinds by having no artistic pretensions. Some half-dozen publishing houses issue them, though the people who draw them seem not to be numerous at any one time.

I have associated them especially with the name of

Donald McGill because he is not only the most prolific and by far the best of contemporary postcard artists, but also the most representative, the most perfect in the tradition. Who Donald McGill is, I do not know. He is apparently a trade name, for at least one series of post-cards is issued simply as 'The Donald McGill Comics', but he is also unquestionably a real person with a style of drawing which is recognizable at a glance. Anyone who examines his postcards in bulk will notice that many of them are not despicable even as drawings, but it would be mere dilettantism to pretend that they have any direct aesthetic value. A comic postcard is simply an illustration to a joke, invariably a 'low' joke, and it stands or falls by its ability to raise a laugh. Beyond that it has only 'ideological' interest. McGill is a clever draughtsman with a real caricaturist's touch in the drawing of faces, but the special value of his postcards is that they are so completely typical. They represent, as it were, the norm of the comic postcard. Without being in the least imitative, they are exactly what comic postcards have been any time these last forty years, and from them the meaning and purpose of the whole genre can be inferred.

Get hold of a dozen of these things, preferably McGill's – if you pick out from a pile the ones that seem to you funniest, you will probably find that most of them are McGill's – and spread them out on a table. What do you see?

Your first impression is of overwhelming vulgarity. This is quite apart from the ever-present obscenity, and apart also from the hideousness of the colours. They have an utter lowness of mental atmosphere which comes out not only in the nature of the jokes but, even more, in the grotesque, staring, blatant quality of the drawings. The designs, like those of a child, are full of heavy lines and empty spaces, and all the figures in them, every gesture and attitude, are deliberately ugly, the faces grinning and vacuous, the women monstrously parodied, with bottoms like Hottentots. Your second impression, however, is of indefinable familiarity. What do these things remind you of? What are they so like? In the first place, of course, they remind you of the barely different postcards which you probably gazed at in your childhood. But more than this, what you are really looking at is something as traditional as Greek tragedy, a sort of sub-world of smacked bottoms and scrawny mothers-in-law which is a part of western European consciousness. Not that the jokes, taken one by one, are necessarily stale. Not being debarred from smuttiness, comic postcards repeat themselves less often than the joke columns in reputable magazines, but their basic subject-matter, the *kind* of joke they are aiming at, never varies. A few are genuinely witty, in a Max Millerish style. Examples:

'I like seeing experienced girls home.'
'But I'm not experienced!'
'You're not home yet!'

'I've been struggling for years to get a fur coat. How did you get yours?' 'I left off struggling.'

Judge: 'You are prevaricating, sir. Did you or did you not sleep with this woman?' Co-respondent: 'Not a wink, my lord!'

In general, however, they are not witty but humorous, and it must be said for McGill's postcards, in particular, that the drawing is often a good deal funnier than the joke beneath it. Obviously the outstanding characteristic of comic postcards is their obscenity, and I must discuss that more fully later. But I give here a rough analysis of their habitual subject-matter, with such explanatory remarks as seem to be needed:

Sex. More than half, perhaps three quarters, of the jokes are sex jokes, ranging from the harmless to the all but unprintable. First favourite is probably the illegitimate baby. Typical captions: 'Could you exchange this lucky charm for a baby's feeding-bottle?' 'She didn't ask me to the christening, so I'm not going to the wedding.' Also newlyweds, old maids, nude statues and women in bathing-dresses. All of these are *ipso facto* funny, mere mention of them being enough to raise a laugh. The cuckoldry joke is very seldom exploited, and there are no references to homosexuality.

Conventions of the sex joke:

a. Marriage only benefits the woman. Every man is plotting seduction and every woman is plotting marriage. No woman ever remains unmarried voluntarily.

b. Sex-appeal vanishes at about the age of twenty-five. Well-preserved and good-looking people beyond their first youth are never represented. The amorous honeymooning couple reappear as the grim-visaged wife and hapless, mustachioed, red-nosed husband, no intermediate stage being allowed for.

Home life. Next to sex, the henpecked husband is the favourite joke. Typical caption: 'Did they get an X-ray of your wife's jaw at the hospital?' – 'No, they got a moving picture instead.'
Conventions:

a. There is no such thing as a happy marriage.
b. No man ever gets the better of a woman in argument.

Drunkenness. Both drunkenness and teetotalism are *ipso facto* funny. Conventions:

a. All drunken men have optical illusions.
b. Drunkenness is something peculiar to middle-aged men. Drunken youths or women are never represented.

W. C. jokes. There is not a large number of these. Chamber-pots are *ipso facto* funny, and so are public lavatories. A typical postcard, captioned 'A Friend in Need', shows a man's hat blown off his head and disappearing down the steps of a ladies' lavatory.

Inter-working-class snobbery. Much in these postcards suggests that they are aimed at the better-off working class and poorer middle class. There are many jokes turning on malapropisms, illiteracy, dropped aitches and the rough manners of slum-dwellers. Countless postcards show draggled hags of the stage-charwoman type exchanging 'unladylike' abuse. Typical repartee: 'I wish you were a statue and I was a pigeon!' A certain number produced since the war treat evacuation from the anti-evacuee angle. There are the usual jokes about tramps, beggars and criminals, and the comic maidservant appears fairly frequently. Also the comic navvy, bargee, etc.; but there are no anti-trade-union jokes. Broadly speaking, everyone with much over or much under £5 a week is regarded as laughable. The 'swell' is almost as automatically a figure of fun as the slum-dweller!

Stock figures. Foreigners seldom or never appear. The chief locality joke is the Scotsman, who is almost inexhaustible. The lawyer is always a swindler, the clergyman always a nervous idiot who says the wrong thing. The 'knut' or 'masher' still appears, almost as in Edwardian days, in out-of-date-looking evening clothes and an opera hat, or even with spats and a knobby cane. Another survival is the Suffragette, one of the big jokes of the pre-1914 period and too valuable to be relinquished. She has reappeared, unchanged in physical appearance, as the Feminist lecturer or Temperance fanatic. A feature of the last few years is the complete absence of anti-Jew postcards. The 'Jew joke', always somewhat more ill-natured than the 'Scotch joke', disappeared abruptly soon after the rise of Hitler.

Politics. Any contemporary event, cult or activity which has comic possibilities (for example, 'free love', feminism, A.R.P., nudism) rapidly finds its way into the picture postcards, but their general atmosphere is extremely old-fashioned. The implied political outlook is a radicalism appropriate to about the year 1900. At normal times they are not only not patriotic, but go in for a mild guying of patriotism, with jokes about 'God save the King', the Union Jack, etc. The European situation only began to reflect itself in them at some time in

1939, and first did so through the comic aspects of A.R.P. Even at this date few postcards mention the war except in A.R.P. jokes (fat woman stuck in the mouth of Anderson shelter; wardens neglecting their duty while young woman undresses at window she had forgotten to black out, etc. etc.). A few express anti-Hitler sentiments of a not very vindictive kind. One, not McGill's, shows Hitler, with the usual hypertrophied backside, bending down to pick a flower. Caption: 'What would *you* do, chums?' This is about as high a flight of patriotism as any postcard is likely to attain. Unlike the twopenny weekly papers, comic postcards are not the product of any great monopoly company, and evidently they are not regarded as having any importance in forming public opinion. There is no sign in them of any attempt to induce an outlook acceptable to the ruling class.

Here one comes back to the outstanding, all-important feature of comic postcards – their obscenity. It is by this that everyone remembers them, and it is also central to their purpose, though not in a way that is immediately obvious.

A recurrent, almost dominant motif in comic postcards is the woman with the stuck-out behind. In perhaps half of them, or more than half, even when the point of the joke has nothing to do with sex, the same female figure appears, a plump 'voluptuous' figure with the dress clinging to it as tightly as another skin and with breasts or buttocks grossly over-emphasized, according to which way it is turned. There can be no doubt that these pictures lift the lid off a very widespread repression, natural enough in a country whose women when young tend to be slim to the point of skimpiness. But at the same time the McGill postcard – and this applies to all other postcards in this genre – is not intended as pornography but, a subtler thing, as a skit on pornography. The Hottentot figures of the women are caricatures of the Englishman's secret ideal, not portraits of it. When one examines McGill's postcards more closely, one notices that his brand of humour only has meaning in relation to a fairly strict moral code. Whereas in papers like *Esquire*, for instance, or *La Vie Parisienne*, the imaginary background of the jokes is always promiscuity, the utter breakdown of all standards, the background of the McGill postcard is marriage. The four leading jokes are nakedness, illegitimate babies, old maids and newly married couples, none of which would seem funny in a really dissolute or even 'sophisticated' society. The postcards dealing with honeymoon couples always have the enthusiastic indecency of those village weddings where it is still considered screamingly funny to sew bells to the bridal bed. In one, for example, a young bridegroom is shown getting out of bed the morning after his wedding night. 'The first morning in our own little home, darling!' he is saying; 'I'll go and get the milk and paper and bring you a cup of tea.' Inset is a picture of the front doorstep; on it are four newspapers and four bottles of milk. This is obscene, if you like, but it is not immoral. Its implication – and this is just the implication that *Esquire* or the *New Yorker* would avoid at all costs – is that marriage is something profoundly exciting and important, the biggest event in the average human being's life. So also with jokes about nagging wives and tyrannous mothers-in-law. They do at least imply a stable society in which marriage is indissoluble and family loyalty taken for granted. And bound up with this is something I noted earlier, the fact that there are no pictures, or hardly any, of good-looking people beyond their first youth. There is the 'spooning' couple and the middle-aged, cat-and-dog couple, but nothing in between. The liaison, the illicit but more or less decorous love-affair which used to be the stock joke of French comic papers, is not a postcard subject. And this reflects, on a comic level, the working-class outlook which takes it as a matter of course that youth and adventure – almost, indeed, individual life – end with marriage. One of the few authentic class-differences, as opposed to class-distinctions, still existing in England is that the working classes age very much earlier. They do not live less long, provided that they survive their childhood, nor do they lose their physical activity earlier, but they do lose very early their youthful appearance. This fact is observable everywhere, but can be most easily verified by watching one of the higher age groups registering for military service; the middle- and upper-class members look, on average, ten years younger than the others. It is usual to attribute this to the harder lives that the working classes have to live, but it is doubtful whether any such difference now exists as would account for it. More probably the truth is that the working classes reach middle age earlier because they accept it earlier. For to look young after, say, thirty is largely a matter of wanting to do so. This generalization is less true of the better-paid workers, especially those who live in council houses and labour-saving flats, but it is true enough even of them to point to a difference of outlook. And in this, as usual, they are more traditional, more in accord with the Christian past than the well-to-do women who try to stay young at forty by means of physical jerks, cosmetics and avoidance of childbearing. The impulse to cling to youth at all costs, to attempt to preserve your sexual attraction, to see even in middle age a future for yourself and not merely for your children, is a thing of recent growth and has only precariously established itself. It will probably disappear again when our standard of living drops and our birth-rate rises. 'Youth's a stuff will not endure' expresses the normal, traditional attitude. It is this ancient wisdom that McGill and his colleagues are reflecting, no doubt unconsciously, when they allow for no transition stage between the honeymoon couple and those glamourless figures, Mum and Dad.

I have said that at least half McGill's postcards are sex jokes, and a proportion, perhaps ten per cent, are far more obscene than anything else that is now printed in England. Newsagents are occasionally prosecuted for selling them, and there would be many more prosecutions if the broadest jokes were not invariably protected by double meanings. A single example will be enough to show how this is done. In one postcard, captioned 'They didn't believe her', a young woman is demonstrating, with her hands held apart, something about two feet long to a couple of open-mouthed acquaintances. Behind her on the wall is a stuffed fish in a glass case, and beside that is a photograph of a nearly naked athlete. Obviously it is not the fish that she is referring to, but this could never be proved. Now, it is doubtful whether there is any paper in England that would print a joke of this kind, and certainly there is no paper that does so habitually. There is an immense amount of pornography of a mild sort, countless illustrated papers cashing in on women's legs, but there is no popular literature specializing in the 'vulgar', farcical aspect of sex. On the other hand, jokes exactly like McGill's are the ordinary small change of the revue and music-hall stage, and are also to be heard on the radio, at moments when the censor happens to be nodding. In England the gap between what can be said and what can be printed is rather exceptionally wide. Remarks and gestures which hardly anyone objects to on the stage would raise a public outcry if any attempt were made to reproduce them on paper. (Compare Max Miller's* stage

* Reviewing *Applesauce*, a variety show, in *Time and Tide*, 7 September 1940, Orwell wrote: 'Anyone wanting to see something really vulgar should visit the Holborn Empire, where you can get quite a good matinée seat for three shillings. Max Miller, of course, is the main attraction.

'Max Miller, who looks more like a Middlesex Street hawker than ever when he is wearing a tail coat and shiny top hat, is one of a long line of English comedians who have specialized in the Sancho Panza side of life, in real *lowness*. To do this probably needs more talent than to express nobility. Little Tich was a master at it. There was a music-hall farce which Little Tich used to act in, in which he was supposed to be factotum to a crook solicitor. The solicitor is giving him his instructions:

'"Now, our client who's coming this morning is a widow with a good figure. Are you following me?"

'*Little Tich:* "I'm ahead of you." '

patter with his weekly column in the *Sunday Dispatch*.)
The comic postcards are the only existing exception to
this rule, the only medium in which really 'low' humour
is considered to be printable. Only in postcards and on
the variety stage can the stuck-out behind, dog and
lamp-post, baby's nappy type of joke be freely exploited.
Remembering that, one sees what function these postcards, in their humble way, are performing.

What they are doing is to give expression to the
Sancho Panza view of life, the attitude to life that Miss
Rebecca West once summed up as 'extracting as much
fun as possible from smacking behinds in basement

'As it happens, I have seen this farce acted several times with other
people in the same part, but I have never seen anyone who could
approach the utter baseness that Little Tich could get into these
simple words. There is a touch of the same quality in Max Miller.
Quite apart from the laughs they give one, it is important that such
comedians should exist. They express something which is valuable
in our civilization and which might drop out of it in certain circumstances. To begin with, their genius is entirely masculine. A woman
cannot be low without being disgusting, whereas a good male comedian can give the impression of something irredeemable and yet
innocent, like a sparrow. Again, they are intensely national. They
remind one how closely knit the civilization of England is, and how
much it resembles a family, in spite of its out-of-date class distinctions.
The startling obscenities which occur in *Applesauce* are only possible
because they are expressed in *doubles entendres* which imply a common
background in the audience. Anyone who had not been brought up
on the *Pink 'Un* would miss the point of them. So long as comedians
like Max Miller are on the stage and the comic coloured postcards
which express approximately the same view of life are in the stationers' windows, one knows that the popular culture of England is
surviving . . .'

kitchens'. The Don Quixote–Sancho Panza combination, which of course is simply the ancient dualism of body and soul in fiction form, recurs more frequently in the literature of the last four hundred years than can be explained by mere imitation. It comes up again and again, in endless variations, Bouvard and Pécuchet, Jeeves and Wooster, Bloom and Dedalus, Holmes and Watson (the Holmes–Watson variant is an exceptionally subtle one, because the usual physical characteristics of two partners have been transposed). Evidently it corresponds to something enduring in our civilization, not in the sense that either character is to be found in a 'pure' state in real life, but in the sense that the two principles, noble folly and base wisdom, exist side by side in nearly every human being. If you look into your own mind, which are you, Don Quixote or Sancho Panza? Almost certainly you are both. There is one part of you that wishes to be a hero or a saint, but another part of you is a little fat man who sees very clearly the advantages of staying alive with a whole skin. He is your unofficial self, the voice of the belly protesting against the soul. His tastes lie towards safety, soft beds, no work, pots of beer and women with 'voluptuous' figures. He it is who punctures your fine attitudes and urges you to look after Number One, to be unfaithful to your wife, to bilk your debts, and so on and so forth. Whether you allow yourself to be influenced by him is a different question. But it is simply a lie to say that he is not part of you, just as it is a lie to say that Don Quixote is not part of you either, though most of what is said and written consists of one lie or the other, usually the first.

But though in varying forms he is one of the stock figures of literature, in real life, especially in the way society is ordered, his point of view never gets a fair hearing. There is a constant world-wide conspiracy to pretend that he is not there, or at least that he doesn't matter. Codes of law and morals, or religious systems, never have much room in them for a humorous view of life. Whatever is funny is subversive, every joke is ultimately a custard pie, and the reason why so large a proportion of jokes centre round obscenity is simply that all societies, as the price of survival, have to insist on a fairly high standard of sexual morality. A dirty joke is not, of course, a serious attack upon morality, but it is a sort of mental rebellion, a momentary wish that things were otherwise. So also with all other jokes, which always centre round cowardice, laziness, dishonesty or some other quality which society cannot afford to encourage. Society has always to demand a little more from human beings than it will get in practice. It has to demand faultless discipline and self-sacrifice, it must expect its subjects to work hard, pay their taxes, and be faithful to their wives, it must assume that men think it glorious to die on the battlefield and women want to wear themselves out with child-bearing. The whole of what one may call official literature is founded on such assumptions. I never read the proclamations of generals before battle, the speeches of fuehrers and prime ministers, the solidarity songs of public schools and left-wing political parties, national anthems, Temperance tracts, papal encyclicals and sermons against gambling and contraception, without seeming to hear in the background a chorus of raspberries from all the millions of common men to whom these high sentiments make no appeal. Nevertheless the high sentiments always win in the end, leaders who offer blood, toil, tears and sweat always get more out of their followers than those who offer safety and a good time. When it comes to the pinch, human beings are heroic. Women face childbed and the scrubbing brush, revolutionaries keep their mouths shut in the torture chamber, battleships go down with their guns still firing when their decks are awash. It is only that the other element in man, the lazy, cowardly, debt-bilking adulterer who is inside all of us, can never be suppressed altogether and needs a hearing occasionally.

The comic postcards are one expression of his point of view, a humble one, less important than the music halls, but still worthy of attention. In a society which is still basically Christian, they naturally concentrate on sex jokes; in a totalitarian society, if they had any freedom of expression at all, they would probably concentrate on laziness or cowardice, but at any rate on the unheroic in one form or another. It will not do to condemn them on the ground that they are vulgar and ugly. That is exactly what they are meant to be. Their whole meaning and virtue is in their unredeemed lowness, not only in the sense of obscenity, but lowness of outlook in every direction whatever. The slightest hint of 'higher' influences would ruin them utterly. They stand for the worm's-eye view of life, for the music-hall world where marriage is a dirty joke or a comic disaster, where the rent is always behind and the clothes are always up the spout, where the lawyer is always a crook and the

Scotsman always a miser, where the newlyweds make fools of themselves on the hideous beds of seaside lodging houses and the drunken, red-nosed husbands roll home at four in the morning to meet the linen-nightgowned wives who wait for them behind the front door, poker in hand. Their existence, the fact that people want them, is symptomatically important. Like the music halls, they are a sort of saturnalia, a harmless rebellion against virtue. They express only one tendency in the human mind, but a tendency which is always there and will find its own outlet, like water. On the whole, human beings want to be good, but not too good, and not quite all the time. For:

there is a just man that perisheth in his righteousness, and there is a wicked man that prolongeth his life in his wickedness. Be not righteous over much; neither make thyself over wise, why shouldest thou destroy thyself? Be not over much wicked, neither be thou foolish: why shouldest thou die before thy time?

In the past the mood of the comic postcard could enter into the central stream of literature, and jokes barely different from McGill's could casually be uttered between the murders in Shakespeare's tragedies. That is no longer possible, and a whole category of humour, integral to our literature till 1800 or thereabouts, has dwindled down to these ill-drawn postcards, leading a barely legal existence in cheap stationers' windows. The corner of the human heart that they speak for might easily manifest itself in worse forms, and I for one should be sorry to see them vanish.

Hop-Picking Diary

25.8.31: On the night of the 25th I started off from Chelsea with about 14/– in hand, and went to Lew Levy's kip in Westminster Bridge Road. It is much the same as it was three years ago, except that nearly all the beds are now a shilling instead of ninepence. This is owing to interference by the L.C.C. who have enacted (in the interests of hygiene, as usual) that beds in lodging houses must be further apart. There is a whole string of laws of this type relating to lodging houses,* but there is not and never will be a law to say that the beds must be reasonably comfortable. The net result of this law is that one's bed is now three feet from the next instead of two feet, and threepence dearer.

26.8.31: The next day I went to Trafalgar Square and camped by the north wall, which is one of the recognized rendezvous of down and out people in London. At this time of year the square has a floating population of 100 or 200 people (about ten per cent of them women), some of whom actually look on it as their home. They get their food by regular begging rounds (Covent Garden at

---

* For instance, Dick's café in Billingsgate. Dick's was one of the few places where you could get a cup of tea for 1d, and there were fires there so that anyone who had a penny could warm himself for hours in the early mornings. Only this last week the L.C.C. closed it on the ground that it was unhygienic [Author's footnote].

4 a.m. for damaged fruit, various convents during the morning, restaurants and dustbins late at night etc.) and they manage to 'tap' likely looking passers by for enough to keep them in tea. Tea is going on the square at all hours, one person supplying a 'drum', another sugar and so on. The milk is condensed milk at 2½d a tin. You jab two holes in the tin with a knife, apply your mouth to one of them and blow, whereupon a sticky greyish stream dribbles from the other. The holes are then plugged with chewed paper, and the tin is kept for days, becoming coated with dust and filth. Hot water is cadged at coffee shops, or at night boiled over watchmen's fires, but this has to be done on the sly, as the police won't allow it. Some of the people I met on the square had been there without a break for six weeks, and did not seem much the worse, except that they are all fantastically dirty. As always among the destitute, a large proportion of them are Irishmen. From time to time these men go home on visits, and it appears that they never think of paying their passage, but always stow away on small cargo boats, the crews conniving.

I had meant to sleep in St Martin's Church, but from what the others said it appeared that when you go in you are asked searching questions by some woman known as the Madonna, so I decided to stay the night in the square. It was not so bad as I expected, but between the cold and the police it was impossible to get a wink of sleep, and no one except a few hardened old tramps even tried to do so. There are seats enough for about fifty people, and the rest have to sit on the ground, which of course is forbidden by law. Every few minutes there would be a shout of 'Look out, boys, here comes the flattie!' and a policeman would come round and shake those who were asleep, and make the people on the ground get up. We used to kip down again the instant he had passed, and this went on like a kind of game from eight at night till three or four in the morning. After midnight it was so cold that I had to go for long walks to keep warm. The streets are somehow rather horrible at that hour; all silent and deserted, and yet lighted almost as bright as day with those garish lamps, which give everything a deathly air, as though London were the corpse of a town. About three o'clock another man and I went down to the patch of grass behind the Guards' parade ground, and saw prostitutes and men lying in couples there in the bitter cold mist and dew. There are always a number of prostitutes in the square; they are the unsuccessful ones, who can't earn enough for their night's kip. Overnight one of these women had been lying on the ground crying bitterly, because a man had gone off without paying her fee, which was sixpence. Towards morning they do not even get sixpence, but only a cup of tea or a cigarette. About four somebody got hold of a number of newspaper posters, and we sat down six or eight on a bench and packed ourselves in enormous paper parcels, which kept us fairly warm till Stewart's café in St Martin's Lane opened. At Stewart's you can sit from five till nine for a cup of tea (or sometimes three or four people even share a cup between them) and you are allowed to sleep with your head on the table till seven; after that the proprietor wakes you. One meets a very mixed crowd there – tramps, Covent Garden porters, early business people, prostitutes – and there are constant quarrels and fights. On this occasion an old, very ugly woman, wife of a porter, was violently abusing two prostitutes, because they could afford a better breakfast than she could. As each dish was brought to them she would point at it and shout accusingly, 'There goes the price of another fuck! *We* don't get kippers for breakfast, do we, girls? 'Ow do you think she paid for them doughnuts? That's that there negro that 'as 'er for a tanner' etc. etc., but the prostitutes did not mind much.

27.8.31: At about eight in the morning we all had a shave in the Trafalgar Square fountains, and I spent most of the day reading *Eugénie Grandet*, which was the only book I had brought with me. The sight of a French book produced the usual remarks – 'Ah, French? That'll be something pretty warm, eh?' etc. Evidently most English people have no idea that there are French books which are not pornographic. Down and out people seem to read exclusively books of the Buffalo Bill type. Every tramp carries one of these, and they have a kind of circulating library, all swapping books when they get to the spike.

That night, as we were starting for Kent the next morning, I decided to sleep in bed and went to a lodging house in the Southwark Bridge Road. This is a seven-penny kip, one of the few in London, and looks it. The beds are five feet long, with no pillows (you use your coat rolled up), and infested by fleas, besides a few bugs. The kitchen is a small, stinking cellar where the deputy sits with a table of flyblown jam tarts etc. for sale a few feet from the door of the lavatory. The rats are so bad that several cats have to be kept exclusively to deal with them. The lodgers were dock workers, I think, and they did not seem a bad crowd. There was a youth among them, pale and consumptive-looking but evidently a labourer, who was devoted to poetry. He repeated

> A voice so thrilling ne'er was 'eard
> In Ipril from the cuckoo bird,
> Briking the silence of the seas
> Beyond the furthest 'Ebrides

with genuine feeling. The others did not laugh at him much.

28.8.31: The next day in the afternoon four of us started out for the hop-fields. The most interesting of the men with me was a youth named Ginger, who is still my mate when I write this. He is a strong, athletic youth of twenty-six, almost illiterate and quite brainless, but daring enough for anything. Except when in prison, he has probably broken the law every day for the last five years. As a boy he did three years in Borstal, came out, married at eighteen on the strength of a successful burglary, and shortly afterwards enlisted in the artillery. His wife died, and a little while afterwards he had an accident to his left eye and was invalided out of the service. They offered him a pension or a lump sum, and of course he chose the lump sum and blued it in about a week. After that he took to burglary again, and has been in prison six times, but never for a long sentence, as they have only caught him for small jobs; he has done one or two jobs which brought him over £500. He has always been perfectly honest towards me, as his partner, but in a general way he will steal anything that is not tied down. I doubt his ever being a successful burglar, though, for he is too stupid to be able to foresee risks. It is all a great pity, for he could earn a decent living if he chose. He has a gift for street selling, and has had a lot of jobs at selling on commission, but when he has had a good day he bolts instantly with the takings. He is a marvellous hand at picking up bargains and can always, for instance, persuade the butcher to give him a pound of eatable meat for twopence, yet at the same time he is an absolute fool about money, and never saves a halfpenny. He is given to singing songs of the Little Grey Home in the West type, and he speaks of his dead wife and mother in terms of the most viscid sentimentality. I should think he is a fairly typical petty criminal.

Of the other two, one was a boy of twenty named Young Ginger, who seemed rather a likely lad, but he was an orphan and had had no kind of upbringing, and lived the last year chiefly on Trafalgar Square. The other was a little Liverpool Jew of eighteen, a thorough guttersnipe. I do not know when I have seen anyone who disgusted me so much as this boy. He was as greedy as a pig about food, perpetually scrounging round dust-bins, and he had a face that recalled some low-down carrion-eating beast. His manner of talking about women, and the expression of his face when he did so, were so loathsomely obscene as to make me feel almost sick. We could never persuade him to wash more of himself than his nose and a small circle round it, and he mentioned quite casually that he had several different kinds of louse on him. He too was an orphan, and had been 'on the toby' almost from infancy.

I had now about 6/–, and before starting we bought a so-called blanket for 1/6d and cadged several tins for 'drums'. The only reliable tin for a drum is a two-pound snuff tin, which is not very easy to come by. We had also a supply of bread and margarine and tea, and a number of knives and forks etc., all stolen at different times from Woolworth's. We took the twopenny tram as far as Bromley, and there 'drummed up' on a rubbish dump, waiting for two others who were to have joined us, but who never turned up. It was dark when we finally stopped waiting for them, so we had no chance to look for a good camping place, and had to spend the night in long wet grass at the edge of a recreation ground. The cold was bitter. We had only two thin blankets between the four of us, and it was not safe to light a fire, as there were houses all round; we were also lying on a slope, so that one rolled into the ditch from time to time. It was rather humiliating to see the others, all younger than I, sleeping quite soundly in these conditions, whereas I did not close my eyes all night. To avoid being caught we had to be on the road before dawn, and it was several hours before we managed to get hot water and have our breakfast.

29.8.31: When we had gone a mile or two we came to an orchard, and the others at once went in and began stealing apples. I had not been prepared for this when we started out, but I saw that I must either do as the others did or leave them, so I shared the apples; I did not however take any part in the thefts for the first day, except to keep guard. We were going more or less in the direction of Sevenoaks, and by dinner time we had stolen about a dozen apples and plums and fifteen pounds of potatoes. The others also went in and tapped whenever we passed a baker's or a teashop, and we got quite a quantity of broken bread and meat. When we stopped to light a fire for dinner we fell in with two Scotch tramps who had been stealing apples from an orchard nearby, and stayed talking with them for a long time. The others all talked about sexual subjects, in a revolting manner. Tramps are disgusting when on this subject, because their poverty cuts them off entirely from women, and their minds consequently fester with obscenity. Merely lecherous people are all right, but people who would like to be lecherous, but don't get the chance, are horribly degraded by it. They remind me of the dogs that hang enviously round while two other dogs are copulating. During the conversation Young Ginger related how he and some others on Trafalgar Square had discovered one of their number to be a 'Poof', or Nancy Boy. Whereupon they had instantly fallen upon him, robbed him of 12/6d, which was all he had, and spent it on themselves. Evidently they thought it quite fair to rob him, as he was a Nancy Boy.

We had been making very poor progress, chiefly because Young Ginger and the Jew were not used to walking and wanted to stop and search for scraps of food all the time. On one occasion the Jew even picked up some chipped potatoes that had been trodden on, and ate them. As it was getting on in the afternoon we decided to make not for Sevenoaks but for Ide Hill spike, which the Scotchmen had told us was better than it is usually represented. We halted about a mile from the spike for tea, and I remember that a gentleman in a car nearby helped us in the kindest manner to find wood for our fire, and gave us a cigarette each. Then we went on to the spike, and on the way picked a bunch of honeysuckle to give to the Tramp Major. We thought this might put him in a good temper and induce him to let us out next morning, for it is not usual to let tramps out of the spike on Sundays. When we got there however the Tramp Major said that he would have to keep us in till Tuesday morning. It appeared that the Workhouse Master was very keen on making every casual do a day's work, and at the same time would not hear of their working on Sunday; so we should have to be idle all Sunday and work on Monday. Young Ginger and the Jew elected to stay till Tuesday, but Ginger and I went and kipped on the edge of a park near the church. It was beastly cold, but a little better than the night before, for we had plenty of wood and could make a fire. For our supper, Ginger tapped the local butcher, who gave us the best part of two pounds of sausages. Butchers are always very generous on Saturday nights.

30.8.31: Next morning the clergyman coming to early service caught us and turned us out, though not very disagreeably. We went on through Sevenoaks to Seal, and a man we met advised us to try for a job at Mitchell's farm, about three miles further on. We went there, but the farmer told us that he could not give us a job, as he had nowhere where we could live, and the Government inspectors had been snouting round to see that all hop-pickers had 'proper accommodation'. (These inspectors,* by the way, managed to prevent some hundreds of unemployed from getting jobs in the hop-fields this year. Not having 'proper accommodation' to offer to pickers, the farmers could only employ local people, who lived in their own houses.) We stole about a pound of raspberries from one of Mitchell's fields, and then went and applied to another farmer called Kronk, who gave us the same answer; we had five or ten pounds of potatoes from his fields, however. We were starting off in the direction of Maidstone when we fell in with an old Irishwoman, who had been given a job by Mitchell on the understanding that she had a lodging in Seal, which she had not. (Actually she was sleeping in a toolshed in somebody's garden. She used to slip in after dark and out before daylight.) We got some hot water from a cottage and the Irishwoman had tea with us, and gave us a lot of food that she had begged and did not want; we were glad of this, for we had now only 2½d left, and none too much food. It had now come on to rain, so we went to a farmhouse beside the church and asked leave to shelter in one of their cowsheds. The farmer and family were just starting out for evening service, and they said in a scandalised manner that of course they could not give us shelter. We sheltered instead in the lych-gate of the church, hoping that by looking draggled and tired we might get a few coppers from the congregation as they went in. We did not get

* Appointed by the Labour Government [Author's footnote].

anything, but after the service Ginger managed to tap a fairly good pair of flannel trousers from the clergyman. It was very uncomfortable in the lych-gate, and we were wet through and out of tobacco, and Ginger and I had walked twelve miles; yet I remember that we were quite happy and laughing all the time. The Irishwoman (she was sixty, and had been on the road all her life, evidently) was an extraordinarily cheerful old girl, and full of stories. Talking of places to 'skipper' in, she told us that one cold night she had crept into a pigsty and snuggled up to an old sow, for warmth.

When night came on it was still raining, so we decided to find an empty house to sleep in, but we went first to buy half a pound of sugar and two candles at the grocer's. While I was buying them Ginger stole three apples off the counter, and the Irishwoman a packet of cigarettes. They had plotted this beforehand, deliberately not telling me, so as to use my innocent appearance as a shield. After a good deal of searching we found an unfinished house and slipped in by a window the builders had left open. The bare floor was beastly hard, but it was warmer than outside, and I managed to get two or three hours' sleep. We got out before dawn, and by appointment met the Irishwoman in a wood nearby. It was raining, but Ginger could get a fire going in almost any circumstances, and we managed to make tea and roast some potatoes.

1.9.31: When it was light the Irishwoman went off to work, and Ginger and I went down to Chambers' farm, a mile or two away, to ask for work. When we got to the farm they had just been hanging a cat, a thing I never heard of anyone doing before. The bailiff said that he thought he could give us a job, and told us to wait; we waited from eight in the morning till one, when the bailiff said that he had no work for us after all. We made off, stealing a large quantity of apples and damsons, and started along the Maidstone road. At about three we halted to have our dinner and make some jam out of the raspberries we had stolen the day before. Near here, I remember, they refused at two houses to give me cold water, because 'the mistress doesn't allow us to give anything to tramps'. Ginger saw a gentleman in a car picnicking nearby, and went up to tap him for matches, for he said, that it always pays to tap from picnickers, who usually have some food left over when they are going home. Sure enough the gentleman presently came across with some butter he had not used, and began talking to us. His manner was so friendly that I forgot to put on my cockney accent, and he looked closely at me, and said how painful it must be for a man of my stamp etc. Then he said, 'I say, you won't be offended, will you? Do you mind taking this?' 'This' was a shilling, with which we bought some tobacco and had our first smoke that day. This was the only time in the whole journey when we managed to tap money.

We went on in the direction of Maidstone, but when we had gone a few miles it began to pour with rain, and my left boot was pinching me badly. I had not had my boots off for three days and had only had about eight hours sleep in the last five nights, and I did not feel equal to another night in the open. We decided to make for West Malling spike, which was about eight miles distant, and if possible to get a lift part of the way. I think we hailed forty lorries before we got a lift. The lorry drivers will not give lifts nowadays, because they are not insured for third party risks and they get the sack if they have an accident. Finally we did get a lift, and were set down about two miles from the spike, getting there at eight in the evening. Outside the gates we met an old deaf tramp who was going to skipper in the pouring rain, as he had been in the spike the night before, and they would confine him for a week if he came again. He told us that Blest's farm nearby would probably give us a job, and that they would let us out of the spike early in the morning if we told them we had already got a job. Otherwise we should be confined all day, unless we went out 'over the wall' – i.e. bolted when the Tramp Major was not looking. Tramps often do this, but you have to cache your possessions outside, which we could not in the heavy rain. We went in, and I found that (if West Malling is typical) spikes have improved a lot since I was last in.* The bathroom was clean and decent, and we were actually given a clean towel each. The food was the same old bread and marg, though, and the Tramp Major got angry when we asked in good faith whether the stuff they gave us to drink was tea or cocoa.† We had beds with straw palliasses and plenty of blankets, and both slept like logs.

In the morning they told us we must work till eleven, and set us to scrubbing out one of the dormitories. As

---

* No: a bit worse if anything [Author's footnote].

† To this day I don't know which it was [Author's footnote].

usual, the work was a mere formality. (I have never done a stroke of real work in the spike, and I have never met anybody who has.) The dormitory was a room of fifty beds, close together, with that warm, faecal stink that you never seem to get away from in the workhouse. There was an imbecile pauper there, a great lump of about sixteen stone, with a tiny, snouty face and a sidelong grin. He was at work very slowly emptying chamberpots. These workhouses seem all alike, and there is something intensely disgusting in the atmosphere of them. The thought of all those grey-faced, ageing men living a very quiet, withdrawn life in a smell of W.C.s, and practising homosexuality, makes me feel sick. But it is not easy to convey what I mean, because it is all bound up with the smell of the workhouse.

At eleven they let us out with the usual hunk of bread and cheese, and we went on to Blest's farm, about three miles away; but we did not get there till one, because we stopped on the way and got a big haul of damsons. When we arrived at the farm the foreman told us that he wanted pickers and sent us up to the field at once. We had now only about 3d left, and that evening I wrote home asking them to send me 10/–; it came two days later, and in the mean time we should have had practically nothing to eat if the other pickers had not fed us. For nearly three weeks after this we were at work hop-picking, and I had better describe the different aspects of this individually.

2.9.31 to 19.9.31: Hops are trained up poles or over wires about 10 feet high, and grown in rows a yard or two apart. All the pickers have to do is to tear them down and strip the hops into a bin, keeping them as clean as possible of leaves. In practice, of course, it is impossible to keep all the leaves out, and the experienced pickers swell the bulk of their hops by putting in just as many leaves as the farmer will stand for. One soon gets the knack of the work, and the only hardships are the standing (we were generally on our feet ten hours a day), the plagues of plant lice, and the damage to one's hands. One's hands get stained as black as a negro's with the hop-juice, which only mud will remove,* and after a day or two they crack and are cut to bits by the stems of the vines, which are spiny. In the mornings, before the cuts had reopened, my hands used to give me perfect agony, and even at the time of typing this (October 10th) they show the marks. Most of the people who go down hopping have done it every year since they were children, and they pick like lightning and know all the tricks, such as shaking the hops up to make them lie loose in the bin etc. The most successful pickers are families, who have two or three adults to strip the vines, and a couple of children to pick up the fallen hops and clear the odd strands. The laws about child labour are disregarded utterly, and some of the people drive their children pretty hard. The woman in the next bin to us, a regular old-fashioned East Ender, kept her grandchildren at it like slaves. – 'Go on, Rose, you lazy little cat, pick them 'ops up. I'll warm your arse if I get up to you' etc. until the children, aged from 6 to 10, used to drop down and fall asleep on the ground. But they liked

* Or hop-juice, funnily enough [Author's footnote].

the work, and I don't suppose it did them more harm than school.

As to what one can earn, the system of payment is this. Two or three times a day the hops are measured, and you are due a certain sum (in our case twopence) for each bushel you have picked. A good vine yields about half a bushel of hops, and a good picker can strip a vine in about 10 minutes, so that theoretically one *might* earn about 30/– by a sixty hour week. But in practice this is quite impossible. To begin with, the hops vary enormously. On some vines they are as large as small pears, and on others hardly bigger than peas; the bad vines take rather longer to strip than the good ones – they are generally more tangled – and sometimes it needs five or six of them to make a bushel. Then there are all kinds of delays, and the pickers get no compensation for lost time. Sometimes it rains (if it rains hard the hops get too slippery to pick), and one is always kept waiting when changing from field to field, so that an hour or two is wasted every day. And above all there is the question of measurement. Hops are soft things like sponges, and it is quite easy for the measurer to crush a bushel of them into a quart if he chooses. Some days he merely scoops the hops out, but on other days he has orders from the farmer to 'take them heavy', and then he crams them tight into the basket, so that instead of getting 20 bushels for a full bin one gets only 12 or 14 – i.e. a shilling or so less. There was a song about this, which the old East End woman and her grandchildren were always singing:

Our lousy hops!
Our lousy hops!
When the measurer he comes round,
Pick 'em up, pick 'em up off the ground!
When he comes to measure
He never knows where to stop;
Ay, ay, get in the bin
And take the fucking lot!

From the bin the hops are put into 10-bushel pokes which are supposed to weigh a hundredweight and are normally carried by one man. It used to take two men to hoist a full poke when the measurer had been taking them heavy.

With all these difficulties one can't earn 30/– a week or anything near it. It is a curious fact, though, that very few of the pickers were aware how little they really earned, because the piece-work system disguises the low rate of payment. The best pickers in our gang were a family of gypsies, five adults and a child, all of whom, of course, had picked hops every year since they could walk. In a little under three weeks these people earned exactly £10 between them – i.e., leaving out the child, about 14/– a week each. Ginger and I earned about 9/– a week each, and I doubt if any individual picker made over 15/– a week. A family working together can make their keep and their fare back to London at these rates, but a single picker can hardly do even that. On some of the farms nearby the tally, instead of being 6 bushels to the shilling, was 8 or 9, at which one would have a hard job to earn 10/– a week.

When one starts work the farm gives one a printed copy of rules, which are designed to reduce a picker more or less to a slave. According to these rules the farmer can sack a picker without notice and on any pretext whatever, and pay him off at 8 bushels a shilling instead of six – i.e. confiscate a quarter of his earnings. If a picker leaves his job before the picking is finished, his earnings are docked the same amount. You cannot draw what you have earned and then clear off, because the farm will never pay you more than two thirds of your earnings in advance, and so are in your debt till the last day. The binmen (i.e. foremen of gangs) get wages instead of being paid on the piecework system, and these wages cease if there is a strike, so naturally they will raise Heaven and earth to prevent one. Altogether the farmers have the hop-pickers in a cleft stick, and always will have until there is a pickers' union. It is not much use to try and form a union, though, for about half the pickers are women and gypsies, and are too stupid to see the advantages of it.

As to our living accommodation, the best quarters on the farm, ironically enough, were disused stables. Most of us slept in round tin huts about 10 feet across with no glass in the windows, and all kinds of holes to let in the wind and rain. The furniture of these huts consisted of a heap of straw and hop-vines, and nothing else. There were four of us in our hut, but in some of them there were seven or eight – rather an advantage, really, for it kept the hut warm. Straw is rotten stuff to sleep in (it is much more draughty than hay) and Ginger and I had only a blanket each, so we suffered agonies of cold for the first week; after that we stole enough pokes to keep us warm. The farm gave us free firewood, though not as much as we needed. The water tap was 200 yards away, and the latrine the same distance, but it was so filthy that one would have walked a mile sooner than use it. There was a stream where one could do some laundering, but getting a bath in the village would have been about as easy as buying a tame whale.

The hop-pickers seemed to be of three types: East Enders, mostly costermongers, gypsies, and itinerant agricultural labourers with a sprinkling of tramps. The fact that Ginger and I were tramps got us a great deal of sympathy, especially among the fairly well-to-do people. There was one couple, a coster and his wife, who were like a father and mother to us. They were the kind of people who are generally drunk on Saturday nights and who tack a 'fucking' on to every noun, yet I have never seen anything that exceeded their kindness and delicacy. They gave us food over and over again. A child would come to the hut with a saucepan: 'Eric, mother was going to throw this stew away, but she said it was a pity to waste it. Would you like it?' Of course they were not really going to have thrown it away, but said this to avoid the suggestion of charity. One day they gave us a whole pig's head, ready cooked. These people had been on the road several years themselves, and it made them sympathetic – 'Ah, I know what it's like. Skippering in the fucking wet grass, and then got to tap the milkman in the morning before you can get a cup of tea. Two of my boys were born on the road' etc. Another man who was very decent to us was an employee in a paper

then pea-picking, strawberries, various other fruits, hops, 'spud-grabbing', turnips and sugar beet. They were seldom out of work for more than a week or two, yet even this was enough to swallow up anything they could earn. They were both penniless when they arrived at Blest's farm, and I saw Barrett work certainly one day without a bite to eat. The proceeds of all their work were the clothes they stood up in, straw to sleep on all the year round, meals of bread and cheese and bacon, and I suppose one or two good drunks a year. George was a dismal devil, and took a sort of worm-like pride in being underfed and overworked, and always tobying from job to job. His line was, 'It doesn't do for people like us to have fine ideas.' (He could not read or write, and seemed to think even literacy a kind of extravagance.) I know this philosophy well, having often met it among the dishwashers in Paris. Barrett, who was 63, used to complain a lot about the badness of food nowadays, compared with what you could get when he was a boy. – 'In them days we didn't live on this fucking bread and marg., we'ad good solid tommy. Bullock's 'eart. Bacon dumpling. Black pudden. Pig's 'ead.' The glutinous, reminiscent tone in which he said 'pig's 'ead' suggested decades of underfeeding.

Besides all these regular pickers there were what are called 'home-dwellers', i.e. local people who pick at odd times, chiefly for the fun of it. They are mostly farmers' wives and the like, and as a rule they and the regular pickers loathe one another. One of them, however, was a very decent woman, who gave Ginger a pair of shoes and me an excellent coat and waistcoat and two shirts.

Most of the local people seemed to look on us as dirt, and the shopkeepers were very insolent, though between us we must have spent several hundred pounds in the village.

One day at hop-picking was very much like another. At about a quarter to six in the morning we crawled out of the straw, put on our coats and boots (we slept in everything else) and went out to get a fire going – rather a job this September, when it rained all the time. By half past six we had made tea and fried some bread for breakfast, and then we started off for work, with bacon sandwiches and a drum of cold tea for our dinner. If it didn't rain we were working pretty steadily till about one, and then we would start a fire between the vines, heat up our tea and knock off for half an hour. After that we were at it again till half past five, and by the time we had got home, cleaned the hop juice off our hands and had tea, it was already dark and we were dropping with sleep. A good many nights, though, we used to go out and steal apples. There was a big orchard nearby, and three or four of us used to rob it systematically, carrying a sack and getting half a hundredweight of apples at a time, besides several pounds of cobnuts. On Sundays we used to wash our shirts and socks in the stream, and sleep the rest of the day. As far as I remember I never undressed completely all the time we were down there, nor washed my teeth, and I only shaved twice a week. Between working and getting meals (and that meant fetching everlasting cans of water, struggling with wet faggots, frying in tin-lids etc.) one seemed to have not an instant to spare. I only read one book all the time I was down there, and that was a Buffalo Bill. Counting up what we spent I find that Ginger and I fed ourselves on about 5/– a week each, so it is not surprising that we were constantly short of tobacco and constantly hungry, in spite of the apples and what the others gave us. We seemed to be forever doing sums in farthings to find out whether we could afford another half ounce of shag or another two-pennorth of bacon. It wasn't a bad life, but what with standing all day, sleeping rough and getting my hands cut to bits, I felt a wreck at the end of it. It was humiliating to see that most of the people there looked on it as a holiday – in fact, it is because hopping is regarded as a holiday that the pickers will take such starvation wages. It gives one an insight into the lives of farm labourers too, to realize that according to their standards hop-picking is hardly work at all.

One night a youth knocked at our door and said that he was a new picker and had been told to sleep in our hut. We let him in and fed him in the morning, after which he vanished. It appeared that he was not a picker at all, but a tramp, and that tramps often work this dodge in the hopping season, in order to get a kip under shelter. Another night a woman who was going home asked me to help her get her luggage to Wateringbury station. As she was leaving early they had paid her off at eight bushels a shilling, and her total earnings were only just enough to get herself and family home. I had to push a perambulator, with one eccentric wheel and loaded with huge packages, two and a half miles through the dark, followed by a retinue of yelling children. When we got to the station the last train was just coming in, and in rushing the pram across the level crossing I upset it. I shall never forget that moment – the train bearing down on us, and the porter and I chasing a tin chamberpot that was rolling up the track. On several nights Ginger tried to persuade me to come and rob the church with him, and he would have done it alone if I had not managed to get it into his head that suspicion was bound to fall on him, as a known criminal. He had robbed churches before, and he said, what surprised me, that there is generally something worth having in the Poorbox. We had one or two jolly nights, on Saturdays, sitting round a huge fire till midnight and roasting apples. One night, I remember, it came out that of about fifteen people round the fire, everyone except myself had been in prison. There were uproarious scenes in the village on Saturdays, for the people who had money used to get well drunk, and it needed the police to get them out of the pub. I have no doubt the residents thought us a nasty vulgar lot, but I could not help feeling that it was rather good for a dull village to have this invasion of cockneys once a year.

19.9.31: On the last morning, when we had picked the last field, there was a queer game of catching the women and putting them in the bins. Very likely there will be something about this in the *Golden Bough*. It is evidently an old custom, and all harvests have some custom of this kind attached to them. The people who were illiterate or therabouts brought their tally books to me and other 'scholars' to have them reckoned up, and some of them paid a copper or two to have it done. I found that in quite a number of cases the farm cashiers had made a mistake in the addition, and invariably the mistake was in favour of the farm. Of course the pickers got the sum due when they complained, but they would not have if they had accepted the farm cashier's reckoning. More- over, the farm had a mean little rule that anyone who was going to complain about his tally book had to wait till all the other pickers had been paid off. This meant waiting till the afternoon, so that some people who had buses to catch had to go home without claiming the sum due to them. (Of course it was only a few coppers in most cases. One woman's book, however, was added up over £1 wrong.)

Ginger and I packed our things and walked over to Wateringbury to catch the hop-pickers' train. On the way we stopped to buy tobacco, and as a sort of fare- well to Kent, Ginger cheated the tobacconist's girl of fourpence, by a very cunning dodge. When we got to Wateringbury station about fifty hoppers were waiting for the train, and the first person we saw was old Deafie, sitting on the grass with a newspaper in front of him. He lifted it aside, and we saw that he had his trousers undone and was exhibiting his penis to the women and children as they passed. I was surprised – such a decent old man, really; but there is hardly a tramp who has not some sexual abnormality. The Hoppers' train was ninepence cheaper than the ordinary fare, and it took nearly five hours to get us to London – 30 miles. At about 10 at night the hop-pickers poured out at London Bridge station, a number of them drunk and all carrying bunches of hops; people in the street readily bought these bunches of hops, I don't know why. Deafie, who had travelled in our carriage, asked us into the nearest pub and stood us each a pint, the first beer I had had in three weeks. Then he went off to Hammersmith, and no doubt he will be on the bum till next year's fruit-picking begins.

On adding up our tally book, Ginger and I found that we had made just 26/– each by eighteen days' work. We had drawn 8/– each in advances (or 'subs' as they are called), and we had made another 6/– between us by selling stolen apples. After paying our fares we got to London with about 16/– each. So we had, after all, kept ourselves while we were in Kent and come back with a little in pocket; but we had only done it by living on the very minimum of everything.

19–9–31 to 8.10.31: Ginger and I went to a kip in Tooley Street, owned by Lew Levy who owns the one in Westminster Bridge Road. It is only sevenpence a night, and it is probably the best sevenpenny one in London. There are bugs in the beds, but not many, and the kitchens, though dark and dirty, are convenient, with abundant fires and hot water. The lodgers are a pretty low lot – mostly Irish unskilled labourers, and out of work at that. We met some queer types among them. There was one man, aged 68, who worked carrying crates of fish (they weigh a hundredweight each) in Billingsgate market. He was interested in politics, and he told me that on Bloody Sunday in '88 he had taken part in the rioting and been sworn in as a special constable on the same day. Another old man, a flower seller, was mad. Most of the time he behaved quite normally, but when his fits were on he would walk up and down the kitchen uttering dreadful beast-like yells, with an expression of agony on his face.

Curiously enough, the fits only came on in wet weather. Another man was a thief. He stole from shop counters and vacant motor cars, especially commercial travellers' cars, and sold the stuff to a Jew in Lambeth Cut. Every evening you would see him smartening himself up to go 'up West'. He told me that he could count on £2 a week, with a big haul from time to time. He managed to swoop the till of a public house almost every Christmas, generally getting £40 or £50 by this. He had been stealing for years and only been caught once, and then was bound over. As always seems the case with thieves, his work brought him no good, for when he got a large sum he blued it instantly. He had one of the ignoblest faces I ever saw, just like a hyena's; yet he was likeable, and decent about sharing food and paying debts.

Several mornings Ginger and I worked helping the porters at Billingsgate. You go there at about five and stand at the corner of one of the streets which lead up from Billingsgate into Eastcheap. When a porter is having trouble to get his barrow up, he shouts 'Up the 'ill!' and you spring forward (there is fierce competition for the jobs, of course) and shove the barrow behind. The payment is 'twopence an up'. They take on about one shover-up for four hundredweight, and the work knocks it out of your thighs and elbows, but you don't get enough jobs to tire you out. Standing there from five till nearly midday, I never made more than 1/6d. If you are very lucky a porter takes you on as his regular assistant, and then you make about 4/6d a morning. The porters themselves seem to make about £4 or £5 a week. There are several things worth noticing about Billingsgate. One is that vast quantities of the work done there are quite unnecessary, being due to the complete lack of any centralised transport system. What with porters, barrow-men, shovers-up etc, it now costs round about £1 to get a ton of fish from Billingsgate to one of the London railway termini. If it were done in an orderly manner, by lorries, I suppose it would cost a few shillings. Another thing is that the pubs in Billingsgate are open at the hours when other pubs are shut. And another is that the barrowmen at Billingsgate do a regular traffic in stolen fish, and you can get fish dirt cheap if you know one of them.

After about a fortnight in the lodging house I found that I was writing nothing, and the place itself was beginning to get on my nerves, with its noise and lack of privacy, and the stifling heat of the kitchen, and above all the dirt. The kitchen had a permanent sweetish reek of fish, and all the sinks were blocked with rotting fish guts which stank horribly. You had to store your food in dark corners which were infested by black beetles and cockroaches, and there were clouds of horrible languid flies everywhere. The dormitory was also disgusting, with the perpetual din of coughing and spitting – everyone in a lodging house has a chronic cough, no doubt from the foul air. I had got to write some articles, which could not be done in such surroundings, so I wrote home for money and took a room in Windsor Street near the Harrow Road. Ginger has gone off on the road again. Most of this narrative was written in the Bermondsey public library, which has a good reading room and was convenient for the lodging house.

NOTES.

New words (i.e. words new to me) discovered this time.

Shackles................broth or gravy.

Drum, a................a billy can. (With verb to drum up meaning to light a fire.)

Toby, on the........on the tramp. (Also to toby, and a toby, meaning a tramp. *Slang Dictionary* gives the toby as the highroad.)

Chat, a..................a louse. (Also chatty, lousy. *S.D.* gives this but not a chat.)

Get, a.....................? (Word of abuse, meaning unknown.)

Didecai, a ....a gypsy.

Sprowsie, a...........a sixpence.

Hard-up................tobacco made from fag ends. (*S.D.* gives a hard-up as a man who collects fag ends.)

Skipper, to.............to sleep out. (*S.D.* gives a skipper as a barn.)

Scrump, to ....to steal.

Knock off, to ....to arrest.

Jack off, to ....to go away.

Jack, on his ....on his own.

Clods ....coppers.

Burglars' slang.

A stick, or a cane.......a jemmy. (*S.D.* gives stick.)

Peter, a ....a safe. (In *S.D.*)

Bly,* a........................an oxy-acetylene blowlamp.

* I forgot to mention that these lamps are hired out to burglars. Ginger said that he had paid £3.10.0 a night for the use of one. So also with other burglars' tools of the more elaborate kinds. When opening a puzzle-lock, clever safe-breakers use a stethoscope to listen to the click of the tumblers [Author's footnote].

Use of the word 'tart' among the East Enders. This word now seems absolutely interchangeable with 'girl', with no implication of 'prostitute'. People will speak of their daughter or sister as a tart.

Rhyming slang. I thought this was extinct, but it is far from it. The hop-pickers used these expressions freely: A dig in the grave, meaning a shave. The hot cross bun, meaning the sun. Greengages, meaning wages. They also used the abbreviated rhyming slang, e.g. 'Use your twopenny' for 'Use your head'. This is arrived at like this: Head, loaf of bread, loaf, twopenny loaf, twopenny.

Homosexual vice in London. It appears that one of the great rendezvous is Charing Cross underground station. It appeared to be taken for granted by the people on Trafalgar Square that youths could earn a bit this way, and several said to me, 'I need never sleep out if I choose to go down to Charing Cross.' They added that the usual fee is a shilling.